The Eye of the Red Dragon

The Guardians of Elestra #5

Thom Jones

Peekaboo Pepper Books

DEDICATION

This book is dedicated to Aidan, whose work on these books has been beyond crucial, Galen, whose guitar playing is quickly becoming the soundtrack to our lives, Dinara, who constantly reminds me how silly kids are, and Linda, who provides a voice of reason when my goofiness gets too obvious in these books.

The Eye of the Red Dragon, Guardians of Elestra #5

Also available in the Guardians of Elestra series:

To learn more about Elestra, including maps, history, Tobungus' blog, Glabber's menu, and contests that allow readers to submit ideas for new characters, places, or other magical things, please visit:

www.guardiansofelestra.com

CONTENTS

1 Buzzy Little Baby

Derek and Deanna Hughes had trouble sleeping for the third straight night. After placing the fourth moonstone in the arch at the top of the Tower of the Moons three days earlier, they had awakened at the same time from separate dreams about their next adventure in Elestra with the words "The Eye of the Red Dragon" escaping their lips. They had become excited and nervous once they realized that they would come face to face with a real dragon. Again on this night, their dreams were filled with quick glimpses of dragons, volcanoes, and oddly enough, mushrooms.

The fifteen moons had all set, and the one Elestran sun was barely peeking above the horizon. Most of the residents of Amemnop were still warm in their beds. Derek pushed the huge window panels open to smell the fresh morning air. The sounds of the magical city caught his attention. He closed his eyes and tried to guess what he was hearing.

The first sound was a series of whooshes, with an occasional honking sound. "The giant geese from the goose-lot," Derek whispered to himself, thinking back on their ride on the huge birds. The next sound was a faint tinkling of running water, cutting through the light breeze. "The fountain," he smiled to himself.

The third sound he could make out was elusive. At first, he heard about ten clicks, then nothing. A few seconds later, twelve more clicks, then silence. Eight more clicks, but this time, a loud note from something that sounded like a kazoo. Derek opened his eyes and saw Deanna looking confused. "What was that?" she asked.

"I have no idea," Derek said. "I was trying to figure out the clicking sound. I think it's getting closer."

Derek was right—the next set of clicks was louder and deeper. He could not quite figure out what it was, but it reminded him of something. It was driving him crazy that he couldn't figure it out. The next clicks were even louder and sounded like something hitting wood.

"Tobungus!" Derek blurted out.

Derek and Deanna peered out the open window and finally found Tobungus, the mushroom man, walking along the wooden sidewalks in his cowboy boots. After a few steps, he stopped, looked down a narrow alley, and blew on a kazoo.

Derek did not want to yell out the window so early in the morning, so he rushed down the stairs, with Deanna right on his heels. She grabbed the Wand of Ondarell and her headband on the way out of the room.

A warm wind whipped their faces as they ran out of Glabber's Grub Hut. It was going to be a hot day in Amemnop.

They caught up with Tobungus, who did not seem to be in any sort of hurry on his strange rounds along the Amemnop store-fronts. "What are you doing?" Deanna asked.

"You wouldn't understand," Tobungus said quickly. He tried to push past the twins and continue his work.

"Try me," Deanna said, standing firm in front of him.

"Okay, okay," he said softly. "I need a new pair of shoes."

"What does that have to do with playing a kazoo?" Derek whispered, laughing under his breath. He should have known that this would have something to do with shoes. One of Tobungus' most treasured possessions was his shoe bag, which held dozens of pairs of shoes. Tobungus regularly changed his shoes in the middle of adventures to create the perfect outfit. Sometimes, it was a pair of cowboy boots, or running shoes, or even tap shoes.

"Just wait," Tobungus answered, looking around. "I suppose that you've never heard of kazoo honey." He saw their blank expressions. "No, I thought not. Well, purple chee-chee bees can't resist kazoo music. When they hear it, they bring their honey and deposit it on the kazoo. Anyway, this honey is more valuable than butter in Elestra. An ounce of purple chee-chee bee honey will fetch enough money for me to get a pair of cleats, with enough left over for a luxurious pair of slippers."

"Why are you looking for these bees here in town?" Deanna asked. "Wouldn't they be out in the country?"

"Well, they have been known to come into town, and I notice that the little girl over there was stung by one earlier," Tobungus said, pointing to his left.

Deanna looked around and saw no one. "Tobungus, what little girl?"

"See that blue mound over there," he answered, pointing to a five foot tall pile of bluish mud. "Chee-chee bee stings are not like most other bee stings. They cover the person who is stung with

a mound of, well, I guess you would call it goo."
He saw their worried expressions. "Don't worry, it
will wear off in a few hours."

"Tobungus," Deanna said worriedly, as a
loud buzzing started up after the latest kazoo blast.
Moments later, a four foot long bee floated out from
between the buildings to their right.

"Oh, look," Tobungus started, "it's a baby.
How cute."

"A baby?" Derek shouted.

Deanna grabbed her brother's hand and
pulled him down the street toward the blue mound.
"Let's get out of here," she yelled.

As they ran, Deanna whipped out the Wand
of Ondarell, muttered a few words and flicked it
toward the girl encased in chee-chee bee goo. A jet
of water hit the bluish mud and exposed a young
girl inside. Within seconds, the little girl was free,
running home to her parents.

Derek looked back and saw an adult bee,
about the size of a small house, gently depositing
several drops of honey on Tobungus' kazoo. He
stopped for a moment, looking at Tobungus and the
enormous bee in disbelief. Then, he turned and
kept running back to Glabber's without looking
back again.

Derek and Deanna found a table at the Grub

Hut and waited for breakfast, while keeping an eye out the window for the massive bees. After a while, the door burst open, and Tobungus walked in, with his short arms outstretched. "The shoe bag's about to get fatter," he exclaimed happily.

Glabber, the snake wizard and owner of the Grub Hut, slithered out to see what was going on. "Call me the Honey King," Tobungus roared. "I got a whole jug of purple chee-chee bee honey."

"My, my," Glabber hissed. "I'll pay the going rate for the whole supply." He slithered back into the kitchen and returned a few moments later with a black velvet bag which he dropped onto the counter.

Tobungus looked inside the bag, and then placed the jug of honey on the counter for Glabber to take. Glabber looked over to the twins, and hissed, "You two are in for a treat."

When their pancakes arrived, Glabber carefully placed one drop of the special honey on each plate.

"Wow," Derek said sarcastically, "Don't go overboard and give us too much or anything."

"You would not be prepared for more than one drop," Glabber said. "Chee-chee bee honey is almost like a magical elixir. You may know that normal honey is a good source of energy. Well, this is ten thousand times more powerful. It will give your bodies amazing power and energy."

Deanna dipped her fork in the honey drop and touched it to her tongue. Instantly, she felt a wave wash over her. Her body tingled. She seemed to hear and see better. Everything felt quicker.

"Now you see," Glabber hissed. "I will give each of you a small vial of the honey to take with you on your adventures, in case of emergencies." He slithered off after giving them their honey.

"When we get back from the picnic, I'm going to get my new shoes," Tobungus squealed.

"The picnic! It's today?" Deanna said excitedly, recalling that one of the King's messengers had appeared as a bird to invite them to a picnic in their honor. "I wonder when we'll have to leave to get to the King's picnic."

"Now should be fine," boomed a deep voice behind them. They turned to see Iszarre stowing his spatula wand in his belt.

"Will we be riding on one of the geese?" Deanna asked. She thought back to their goose ride to the Forest of Confusion on their way to finding the second moonstone in the Baroka Valley.

"No, we'll use magic," Iszarre answered.

"Are you trying to tell me that the geese that change from normal sized birds into giant flying transports are not magical?" Deanna asked.

"Oh, of course, you're right," Iszarre replied, "but we'll be using something new." He led them into the street.

"Something new?" Derek asked.

"Indeed," Iszarre said. "I've come up with my own method of travel that should prove interesting. Now, if that cat would just show up."

"Interesting? Wait! You've done this before, haven't you?" Derek asked.

Iszarre was searching up and down the street. "Iszarre," Derek said more loudly, "have you tried this new type of travel yet?"

"What," the wizard said absent-mindedly. "Oh, yes, I've already tried it, and it works perfectly." Just then, Zorell, the talking cat that traded insults with Tobungus constantly, ran up to the group.

"Will it just be you, or will the fleas be coming too?" Tobungus asked.

Pretending not to hear, Zorell said, "Is the King aware that we will be bringing mold spores with us."

"Can't this bickering wait until after lunch?" Deanna asked, with her hand resting on her wand. Tobungus and Zorell instantly became quiet.

Iszarre pulled out a thick rubber cord with a

ball at one end and something that looked like a cup at the other end. "Alright, the idea here is that this cup-like end will expand and act as a carriage. I'll throw the ball through a magical tunnel that I will open up, and the carriage will whip forward as the rubber snaps toward the ball. Easy! Nothing to it."

Iszarre pulled out his spatula and waved it at the air in front of him. A swirling patch of orange light grew larger and brighter, eventually opening into a tunnel that was so long that they couldn't see the other end. He touched the cup end of the rubber device, and it grew into a bowl at least five feet across. He threw the ball end through the tunnel, and jumped into bowl, with his spatula waving at the others. They all rose from the ground and landed with him in the bowl.

"You're sure you've done this before?" Derek asked, as the bowl began to move toward the tunnel.

"Yes," Iszarre answered. "Well, sort of. Actually, I haven't ridden in it. I used it to send a few bales of hay to a friend's donkey stables."

"Iszarre!" Derek yelled, as the bowl snapped suddenly into the tunnel. They were traveling faster than any of them could imagine. They could barely make out trees, rivers, and mountains passing under them. Then, everything was dark, as they flew across the space between Elestra and one of the moons. Before they knew it, the light returned, and they were thrown out of the bowl, and into the upper branches of a huge tree.

"How do we get down?" Deanna groaned, looking at the ground, hundreds of feet below them. Before she could grab her wand and try some sort of levitation spell, several of the branches began to move. The leafy arms grabbed the twins and their fellow travelers and carefully placed them on the ground.

Deanna's mouth was hanging open as she turned to say something to Iszarre.

"Thank you," the old wizard said, to the tree. "I'm starved. Let's get to that picnic."

2 Royal Picnic

The first odd thing about the grounds of King Barado's Castle was that nothing looked odd. Derek and Deanna both noticed it. There were no giant chickens, oozing slugfruit trees, monstrous bees, or any of the other things that made Elestra frightening and enchanting at the same time. The tree had put them down in a meadow outside the walls of the castle's grounds. Iszarre was hurrying to the massive gate that would lead to their first meeting with the great king.

Giant chains holding the gate closed creaked as the slab of wood lowered. Derek and Deanna held their breath, not knowing what to expect. They exhaled and followed Iszarre inside the fortress.

While the meadow outside had looked perfectly normal, the grounds inside the wall looked as bizarre as they could imagine. Bushes chased miniature sand dunes, throwing berries that they picked from their own branches. A dog with droopy jowls blew bubbles from a pipe and told a gold skinned fairy about his favorite type of math. A family of four rainbow colored balls forced a clown to juggle them.

Mermaids raced sea serpents in the moat, while a group of young cloud creatures played hide and seek in and out of the trees along its bank.

Deanna stared in disbelief at the barrage of images. She was just able to understand one new sight, when five more came into view. The feeling was overwhelming, and was not cured by a booming voice that said, "You must be Deanna. I've been waiting to meet you in person."

Deanna looked up to see King Barado towering over the group. He must have been at least fifteen feet tall. He saw her reaction which was more fear than excitement. "Oh, sorry," he said. "I really should work on my entrance." He pulled out a wand and flicked it at himself. He shrunk down to a normal adult size. "I have to use that growth spell when leaders of the various realms visit, and I forgot to change back."

"You've had visitors," Iszarre cut in. "We don't wish to interrupt important business."

"No, Paramage," Barado said, with a slight bow, "I am always happy to see you, and I can't think of any more important visitors than our young Mystical Guardians. Besides, I have finished my dealings with the Dragons. Their leaders are heading back soon."

Derek swelled with pride, thinking that he and Deanna were more interesting and important than dragons. "We have been dying to meet you, sir," Derek said. "So many people in Elestra are hoping that you can defeat Eldrack and make sure that Elestra will have peace."

"Young Derek," Barado said, "I, too, hope for an end to the fighting and look forward to Eldrack's defeat. You and your sister have done so much to make sure that we are successful. You have stood up to Eldrack again and again, and never given in. He is a cunning sorcerer who has defeated powerful wizards. You should be proud of your work."

"It's not that simple, Your Majesty," Deanna began, thinking about her confusion over Eldrack's actions and the fact that he seemed to protect her from getting crushed under Tarook's Temple while she was retrieving the fourth moonstone, but saw that Iszarre barely shook his head as if to tell her to stop.

"What do you mean, Deanna?" Barado asked.

"Oh," she said, "it's just that we have so much more to do. So many more moonstones to find. We feel lucky with every battle, and I hope that we don't run out of luck."

"Luck has very little to do with it," Barado

said with a smile. "Your power is, well, it's something that Elestra has never seen before." He glanced at Iszarre who said nothing.

"What do you mean?" Deanna asked.

"Deanna," Barado said, putting his hand on her shoulder, "there have been many powerful wizards in Elestra's history, but they have all studied the magical arts for years, decades really, before they are able to use a wand like you have been able to. You have a power that defies the understanding of most who study magic here."

Derek listened to Barado's words and looked at Iszarre who was staring expressionless at the king. Something about Iszarre's look told him that there was something deeper about Deanna's power that he would have to uncover.

"And now, Deanna and Derek, my honored guests, it is time for us to have our picnic," the king said. He led the group to a sunny patch and waved his wand toward the castle. Dozens, if not hundreds, of flying fairies and elven chefs swarmed out of the giant stone building, carrying every imaginable type of food. Tables appeared out of thin air, plates floated down from the tops of trees, and fountains of exotic juices sprang up from the ground.

Everyone began filling their plates at once.

Iszarre was very picky, sampling tiny bites here and there, scratching his head with his wooden spoon, as if he were trying to figure out the recipes. Derek had a towering plate of food, while Deanna kept getting tiny servings of each dish.

Zorell was lying down with a massive fish, eating huge mouthfuls as quickly as he could. Before long, he was so stuffed that he could hardly move, but he wanted to keep eating. A small army of tiny fairies carried bites of the fish to the sprawled cat who half purred/half burped between each bite.

Tobungus gnawed on a soft brown branch that looked like it had been sitting on a forest floor for years. Seeing Derek's look of confusion, he said, "We mushroom people can get a lot of nutrients from decaying wood. Plus, it's covered in some type of gravy that makes it irresistible. Do you want a bite?"

"No, thanks," Derek said. "I'll just stick to my plate of non-decaying food."

After everyone was full, King Barado stood and addressed the group, "I must go in and attend to the desserts that will be brought out. Please, feel free to explore the castle grounds while I am gone." He turned and hurried inside the castle with the chefs.

Derek waited a few moments to make sure that the king was gone. Then, he looked around the castle grounds to see where Iszarre had wandered off to. He saw Iszarre at the edge of a grove of fruit trees.

Derek told Deanna that he was going to ask Iszarre about the mermaids. As Derek got closer to the trees, he realized that Iszarre was arguing with one of the trees about giving him a peach.

"Iszarre?" Derek said quietly.

Iszarre turned, with peach juice running down his chin. "Ah, yes, Derek." The old wizard seemed to be expecting him.

"I was wondering about something," Derek continued. Iszarre looked him in the eyes. At first, Derek couldn't concentrate with this great wizard staring at him, looking like a little child with peach juice all over his face and shirt. "I was wondering about what Barado said about Deanna's power."

"Derek, you have seen how Deanna uses the wand. She has a natural gift for magic."

"I know that," Derek said. "I love how great she is with magic. She's saved us a bunch of times. What I'm wondering about is about how he said that her power is so unusual, how no one has seen it in such a young wizard."

"Yes, that is what the king said," Iszarre

replied quickly.

"Yes, but I got the feeling that there was more to the story," Derek said.

Iszarre sighed, as if he were not sure that he wanted to talk about this subject with Derek. "Okay, Derek," he said. "It is very unusual to see this level of magical power in someone so young, but it is not completely unheard of. There was another wizard who displayed great power at a young age. Many older wizards worried that such a young wizard would not be able to control such power and would fall into the trap of darkness that hides under the surface of magic."

"Did the other wizard become a dark wizard?" Derek asked.

"I'm not sure," Iszarre answered carefully. "And now," he stated dramatically, changing the subject, "you must get back to the picnic, and I must convince this stubborn tree to give up another peach."

Derek still had more questions than answers, but he could tell from Iszarre's tone that the wizard had told him all that he would, for the moment. There was one thing that he had to ask before leaving Iszarre to his battle with the peach tree. "Iszarre, what about sending a message to our parents?

The messenger who invited them to the picnic had told Derek and Deanna that King Barado decided that they could use the screaming newts to call their parents while at the castle.

Iszarre turned back to Derek. "I know King Barado's messenger said you would be able to contact your parents, but I told Barado that I don't think that would be a good idea. I'm afraid that Eldrack could find a way to trace the message to your parents' exact location.

Derek started to argue. He really had hoped to talk to his mom and dad.

But, Iszarre held up his hand. "When the time is right, I'll help you contact your parents." Iszarre looked very serious, but he had a spark in his eye that made Derek think that he already had a plan to call their parents.

"Thanks, Iszarre," Derek said. He let Iszarre get back to his quest for another peach and returned to the party. On his way, he ran into Deanna who was walking along a path near the moat.

"Hey, Derek," she said, "What's the story on the mermaids?"

"Hmm, oh, Iszarre wasn't too clear on that," Derek said, hoping she wouldn't ask too many questions. He wasn't ready to tell her the real reason he had wanted to talk to Iszarre. He was about to try to change the subject, when a lumbering group of dragons did it for him.

Three green dragons, each at least thirty feet tall, walked toward the gate with serious looks. A smaller green dragon, who looked younger, followed behind. "Come on Olvard," the last of the large green dragons roared.

"Coming," the younger dragon said in a quiet voice. He looked over and was surprised to see the twins. "Oh, my," he said.

"Hello," Deanna said. "I'm sorry if we startled you. We've never met a dragon before."

"Oh, well, it's nice to meet you," Olvard said. "I wish I had more time to talk with you, but I have to get back to my realm."

"Olvard! Come on!" the largest of the green dragons boomed in an angry voice.

Olvard sucked in his breath and whispered, "I'm the King of the Dragon Realm. I should get to decide how quickly I move." Before the other dragons could say anything further, he called out to them, "I'm on my way!"

The other dragons snorted, as if they were tired of taking care of the smaller dragon.

"That wasn't very nice," Deanna said to Derek, after the dragons had left.

"Yeah, and it's too bad he wasn't red," Derek

said. "It would have made our next adventure a lot easier."

They walked further along the path which wound back around to the picnic area. By the time they got there, King Barado was finishing the preparations for the desserts. A ten foot tall cake shot tiny fountains of chocolate sauce that flowed down its sixty layers. A group of brightly colored cupcakes pushed each other around and shouted, "Pick me!" Giant spiders in clown costumes carried a variety of fruit and cream pies in each of their many arms.

Zorell couldn't believe his eyes when he saw a fish cupcake and gladly picked it as his dessert. Tobungus drank chocolate sauce from the side of the cake with a straw and shoved candied peekaboo peppers in his mouth between sips.

Everyone spent another hour stuffing themselves on sweets before saying "Goodbye" to King Barado and heading back to the gate for their trip back to Amemnop. King Barado thanked them again, wished them luck, and declared that they would always be welcome to visit his castle.

The slingshot ride back was not as scary, but it was nauseating after eating so much.

The sun was setting when they returned to the Grub Hut, and they dragged themselves up the stairs to their room, not wanting to think about eating anything else until morning.

Before going to sleep, Deanna said, "Derek, what did you really talk to Iszarre about?"

"Wow, you are good," Derek replied. "I just wanted to get his version of Barado's story about your power."

"Derek," Deanna said, "You have great power too." She was thinking that Derek was jealous of her magical abilities.

"No, Deanna, don't get me wrong," he said. "It looked like Iszarre wanted to say something when Barado was talking. He wouldn't go into detail, but I've been thinking, and I think that I figured it out."

"What is it?" Deanna asked.

"I think that there was another wizard who became powerful at a very young age, and I think that this wizard gave in to the darkness." He looked at Deanna. "I think the other wizard was Eldrack."

3 Narrow Your Search

Derek and Deanna got up early and headed to the State Library of Magia alone. Tobungus set off on a quest to buy his cleats and slippers. Zorell visited shops along the boardwalk, gathering items to bring to the Dragon Realm. On their way, they had to duck into an alley to avoid a group of kids using overly ripe slugfruits like water balloons. The gray goo from the slugfruits covered the kids' clothing, the streets, and an old man who seemed very interested in a line of insects carrying garden fairies along the sidewalk. He did not know that the fairies paid the insects for the ride because the wooden sidewalks tickled their tiny feet.

When they had passed through the giant doors to the Library, Deanna walked over to the six inch tall librarian and asked for books about dragons. There was a deafening buzzing as the wings of every book fairy in the Library shot out from hidden nooks and crannies.

"Stop!" the librarian shouted to the fairies. Turning to Deanna, she said, "I'm sorry, young lady, but you will have to narrow your search. If we get all books on dragons, half of the Library will come raining down on you."

"How about the Dragon Realm?" Deanna asked in a whisper so that the book fairies could not hear.

"No, still too broad," the tiny woman replied.

"Then, the Red Dragon," Derek cut in.

"Yes, that should be more reasonable," the librarian said. She turned to the empty air above them and shouted, "Bring books that talk about the Red Dragon to table six."

The book fairies swarmed out, but now there were only about twenty. Within seconds, the books spiraled down and came to a rest on the table where Derek and Deanna had set their bags. The librarian glided over to their table and said, "you'll have to be firm with the books today. They are angry about not getting a holiday that was promised to them by the last librarian."

Derek looked at the librarian as she left. He didn't know what to say. He had never heard of books being angry before, and even though he had seen many strange creatures in Elestra, the idea of angry books was too bizarre for him to comprehend.

He did not have to wait long to see what an angry book would look like, however. The first book that Deanna questioned said, "No!" the first several times she said anything. Then, it started saying, "La La La," to drown her out.

She pulled out the Wand of Ondarell and said, "*Silencio*," which stopped the book from talking, but it still would not cooperate. She was getting frustrated and tried to figure out how to make a stubborn book talk.

"Tell it you'll give it something," Derek suggested.

"Give it what?" Deanna asked.

Derek looked around and saw the sea of books on the shelves all around them. He realized that even though the books were being stubborn, they loved having people read them. Derek moved closer to the book and said, "Some of the other books here have helped us on our missions." He waited a few seconds, and then added, "You do know that we're Mystical Guardians, don't you?"

"Yes, I know that," the book answered.

Derek smiled. "Well, when we finish all of our missions, I'm sure that there will be new books that tell the stories of our adventures."

"Yes, so?" the book replied grumpily.

"So, the books that help us on our quests will be mentioned in those books. Think about it. You'd be famous." Derek paused, letting his words sink in.

The book opened its cover and said, "How can I help you?"

"Tell me about the Red Dragon," Deanna said quickly before the book could change its mind.

The book recited a passage about the Red Dragon, saying:

> "The Red Dragon is the form taken by the strongest and bravest Dragon Kings. When a Dragon King comes to power, he is green, like most dragons in the Dragon Realm. After he reaches the age of ascension, he enters the volcanic pit of Mt. Infernus. He faces trials that test his intelligence, his bravery, and his strength.
>
> During the trials, the King's body is transformed by the heat of the magma, and his final color is determined by his successes and failures within the volcano.
>
> Most Dragon Kings are yellow. Some are orange. Very few are red, the color of the most powerful rulers. The last Red Dragon was Telgaar, over two hundred years ago. Since then, all Dragon Kings have been yellow, except for Sorbard the Orange. The current king is Olvard who is nearing the age of ascension."

Deanna asked Derek if he wanted to use the wand to read from another book, but he thought that she knew more spells to use on the disobedient books, so he said that he would just sit back and listen. Before she could get the next book to talk, a tattered piece of parchment floating from the ceiling caught Derek's attention. He watched it wafting on air currents around the room, slowly dropping past one shelf after another. The single page finally landed on the table in front of him.

Derek looked around to see if anyone had used some simple spell to make the paper come to him, but he saw no one. He decided to see what it said, so he leaned forward and read to himself:

"Magical Arts, Lesson 1. Most students of magic want to learn spells to cast on objects and people, but they do not realize that magic has two parts. Using spells is the offensive side of magic. When casting a spell, magic travels away from the wizard. There is also defensive magic which is used to protect oneself against magical spells. When using defensive spells, magic travels to the wizard. The strongest wizards absorb the magical power of their enemies' spells and make their own spells more powerful.

Wizards usually start with equal offensive

and defensive magical abilities, but they can make one stronger than the other with practice. The strongest wizards have very high offensive and defensive powers.

Bandrakkus, the great wizard teacher, has discovered that offensive and defensive powers are rather mysterious in twins. It seems that one twin . . ."

The page ended there. Derek turned the page over to see if there was any writing on the other side, but it was blank.

"Derek, are you paying attention?" Deanna asked. She saw that he was looking around, as if he was trying to find someone.

"Hmm? Oh, yeah, sorry," Derek answered. He really was not listening to Deanna or the book she chose. He was more interested in what Bandrakkus had found out about twins. He was also curious about who had made the mysterious page float down to him.

Deanna returned to the book, but said to Derek, "Good, because this book tells us what we need to know about the Dragon Realm." The book read aloud,

"One of the Six Kingdoms of Elestra, the

Sky Dragons or Dragon Realm, is considered nearly as powerful as Magia. The Dragon Realm is located around the arc of volcanic mountains far south of Magia. The Dragons get their physical strength and magical abilities from the magical well water that seeps up through the magma chambers of the volcanoes and emerges as steam. The dragons breathe the steam and grow more powerful.

The well water erupts as geysers when the volcanoes erupt, and the lava that is blown high into the sky has hardened into floating islands in the clouds. There are many island provinces that all are loyal to the King of the Dragon Realm. The dragons are generally peaceful, and friendly, but they tend to stay in their Realm because most other places in Elestra are too cold for them. They occasionally take vacations to Mt. Cauldron and splash around in the River of the Dragon's Breath.

The Dragon Realm has seen two hundred years of peace after King Telgaar united the floating island states. But, over the past five years, there have been rumors that some of the island states have been preparing to rise up and take control of the Dragon Realm, but nothing has happened yet."

Derek thought through what he had just heard and asked, "Have we figured out how to get there yet?"

"Here's an atlas of Elestra," Deanna said. "This ought to help." She was ready to do battle with another book and started by touching the wand to the book's cover and saying "*Explanatum*."

She was surprised when the book said, "I'm ready to help a wizard in need. I'm not like those other books that whine about vacations and holidays. Day and night, it's nothing but complaining since that new librarian came."

"I like the new librarian," the book continued happily. "She has the book fairies give us regular dusting with extra large feather dusters made from the feathers of the Garpesian Leopard Owl. Sooooo Soft!"

"Oh, thank you," Deanna said. "We need to know how to get to the Dragon Realm."

The book explained:

"Magia lies in a strip around the center of Elestra. The Dragon Realm is located at the far southern tip of Elestra. You can reach it by air, sea, or land. Travel by air is dangerous because you may run into Hurricane Delmar. Delmar was a crazy old wizard who liked to throw things

at travelers. Paramage Quantark turned him into a cloud as punishment, but he got angry and grew into a hurricane. Now he floats around and throws boats, rain, whales, and anything else he can drum up at people.

Travel by sea is easy from the far side of Magia, but from Amemnop it is difficult because you would have to find your way through the Maze Sea. To make it worse, the only way into the Maze Sea is guarded by trolls who make travelers wear magical blindfolds that stay on until you reach the center of the maze.

That leaves travel by land which means that you must pass through the Torallian Forest. Once you are past the forest, head to the town of Grup where you can arrange for passage to the capital of the Dragon Realm."

"Oh, great," Derek sighed.

"What's wrong?" Deanna asked.

"The Torallian Forest," Derek began, "Tobungus is from the Torallian Forest. Imagine hundreds or thousands of people like Tobungus."

"Ooh, that will be interesting," Deanna laughed. Then, she thought for a moment and laughed ever harder, "Zorell won't be happy about this."

4 Home Sweet Home

Derek and Deanna went straight back to Glabber's to pick up Tobungus and Zorell. When they walked through the swinging doors to the Grub Hut, they saw Zorell sitting on a nearby table with a blindfold over his eyes. Tobungus was nowhere to be seen.

"Zorell," Derek said, sitting down next to him, "what's with the blindfold?"

"I'd rather not think about what today will be like," the cat answered. "Now, if you'll excuse me, I'm trying to think happy thoughts."

"Happy thoughts for you surely include dancing pieces of string, a fresh litter box, and a tasty mouse," the familiar voice of Tobungus chimed in from behind the counter. The mushroom man emerged from the kitchen with a small pitcher of red liquid.

"Ommmmm," Zorell chanted, trying to put himself in a trance.

"Tobungus, what are you doing back there?" Deanna asked.

"My tap shoes just won't do it, Deanna," he

replied. "And, even though I love my new cleats and slippers, those are not right for this occasion."

"And what does that have to do with the kitchen?" Derek asked.

"I had to get a nice drink for my hiking shoes," Tobungus said. Derek and Deanna just looked at him. "You two have so much to learn. Here." He reached into his shoe bag and pulled out a box shaped like a small house. He carefully pulled out a pair of shoes that seemed to be breathing. "Okay my babies, I got you some nice flipper juice."

"Did you just call a pair of shoes your babies?" Derek laughed.

"He sure did," Zorell said, lifting the blindfold off of one eye. "There's probably some resemblance between the inside of old shoes and an oversized fungus."

"Tobungus," Derek continued, "don't tell me that flipper juice is something squeezed out of some bizarre animal's flipper."

"Don't be ridiculous," Tobungus said. "The hulking sea squirrel uses its flipper to slap the fruit of the bush of stubbornness until a thick juice comes out. That's flipper juice, and my shoes love it." He carefully poured the juice into the shoes which started to hop around the table. "Okay, okay, wait until I put you on."

Tobungus put the now burping shoes on his feet and instantly started a super-fast twitchy dance, yelling "yee-ha" the whole time.

"This is just the start," Zorell moaned. "He knows that we're going to the Torallian Forest, so he's celebrating with this wiggling mess that he calls a dance."

The dance continued for almost an hour, with Tobungus stopping every five minutes to feed the shoes more flipper juice.

Finally, the shoes began to slow their dance and then snoring could be heard, coming from Tobungus' feet. Tobungus dropped into the chair next to Deanna, took a long swig of thick, brown mulch juice, and announced that he was ready to head out.

The group left Glabber's and headed to the carriage station on the south side of Amemnop. Iszarre had suggested that they ride in a carriage that was pulled by a swarm of dragonflies to save time on their journey.

The carriage turned out to be the cracked open egg of the mostly featherless hermit bird. At Derek's and Deanna's looks of amazement, Zorell explained, "The hermit bird's egg is a normal size for an egg when it is first laid, but is the size of a small car by the time the "chick" finally hatches. Hermit birds often remain in their eggs for ten years after the egg is laid. The egg continues to grow as the bird grows."

Tobungus nodded and added, "Hermit birds are very shy and lay their eggs in areas overrun by curious insects such as the appropriately named crunchy beetle. The bird makes a small hole in the egg and the insects come inside, only to be eaten by the reclusive bird. After ten years, the hermit birds usually decide that it's time for a vacation, so they crack open their shells and fly off to tan their bizarre featherless bodies on the shores of Lake Gawk."

The egg carriage was large and very comfortable. The beating of the dragonflies' wings was a relaxing background tune for the smooth ride. Derek and Deanna spent the first hour looking out the windows at the beautiful scenery that went from marshes, to forests, and then to prairie. Tobungus looked like he was going to burst with excitement as a line of bushes appeared on the horizon. Within a half hour, they arrived at the edge of the Torallian forest.

"Beautiful, isn't it?" Tobungus asked everyone in the group.

"Tobungus," Deanna said, "the trees are only about four feet tall. It's more like a sea of bushes."

"No, Deanna," Tobungus said seriously, "the Torallian Forest is grand. When we enter, you will understand." He looked around near the base of a small tree that looked like it belonged on someone's desk. "Ah, Dumott, there you are."

"Tobungus," a squeaky voice said, "what brings you back home?" Derek squinted and finally figured out that Tobungus was talking to another mushroom man, only this one was the size of a regular mushroom that someone might find in their kitchen.

"I am traveling with the new Mystical Guardians, and we need to visit the dragons," Tobungus answered proudly.

"Ooh, very nice," Dumott said. "Will it be the whole bunch of you going through today, then?"

"Yes, we all have to transform," Tobungus said.

"Transform?" Derek said as the tiny Dumott waved a sliver of a twig that Derek figured was a miniature wand. Before he could ask Tobungus what he meant about transforming, he felt as if a giant hand squeezed him gently. The trees seemed to grow in an instant, and he looked at Deanna whose eyes were wide with surprise, and maybe a little fear.

Derek realized that the trees hadn't grown. Dumott had shrunk them all down to about an inch tall. The trees towered over them, and the Torallian Forest now looked majestic.

"Tobungus," Deanna said, "you're probably about as big now as when we first got you." She thought back to Aramaltus who had given the twins a red striped mushroom that turned out to be Tobungus.

"Indeed, I am," Tobungus said. "After my earlier travels with Nibblebits and his handlers, er family, I had to come back to heal my cuts and drink lots of calming oboongoo tea. After I had found peace in this paradise, I volunteered to serve King Barado. The king allowed Iszarre to decide where I was needed most. Iszarre decided that I should wait for an important mission in the forest with Aramaltus."

He took a deep breath and continued, "Our patron wizard used the long-night spell to keep me in a deep sleep until I was called on to help. Then, you came along and knocked on my cap to wake me up."

Tobungus thanked Dumott and led the way deeper into the forest. He promised to take the shortest route to the other side, so that they would reach the Dragon Realm as quickly as possible.

After a while, another mushroom man called Tobungus' name and started running to catch up with them.

"Rorrdoogo," Tobungus called out with a smile. He turned to Derek and whispered, "he's a lunatic."

Derek thought about how bizarre Rorrdoogo must be if Tobungus thought he was strange. After meeting Rorrdoogo, Derek decided that "bizarre" only began to describe him. Rorrdoogo started and ended every sentence with a loud snort, and interrupted himself for a vigorous argument on the meaning of the word drip.

"Where's my blindfold?" Zorell muttered to himself.

"Zorell, just keep an eye out for danger," Deanna whispered to the unhappy cat. Zorell was happy to have been given an excuse to move out of range of the two mushroom men and to keep his mind off of the hundreds or thousands of Tobungus' people who were all around him.

After welcoming Tobungus back to the forest, Rorrdoogo turned to Derek and Deanna and eagerly introduced himself. Derek made the mistake of asking the strange newcomer how he was doing.

"Miserably," Rorrdoogo answered. "My

business is not going well, and I think that I will have to start giving away free samples."

"Free samples of what?" Derek asked.

"I'll show you. Wait a second," Rorrdoogo said. "What do you want?"

Derek thought for a moment. It was a little cold, and he was hungry. "How about soup?" Derek replied.

"Okay," Rorrdoogo squeaked. He waved his twig-like wand. "There you go."

"What do you mean?" Derek asked. He expected to see a bowl of soup, but nothing had appeared.

"You're now allergic to soup," Rorrdoogo said proudly.

"What?" Derek blurted out. "Why would you make me allergic to soup?"

"As I said, I am giving away free samples of what I sell, and what I sell are allergies," Rorrdoogo said.

"But, but, but," Derek sputtered.

"Now you're saying you don't want a soup allergy?" Rorrdoogo asked. "Fine, I can reverse it." He waved his wand again, and said, "It will take a couple of days to wear off, and until then, you have what I might describe as a super-allergy to soup. Trust me, order a salad or sandwich if you go to a restaurant."

Derek backed away from Rorrdoogo without saying anything. He was trying to figure out how it was possible that Tobungus was not the strangest creature he had ever met.

The next person that Derek and Deanna met was the Mushroom Wizard Bohootus who seemed fairly normal to the twins. He didn't change his shoes once while they spoke with him, he didn't offer free samples of allergies, and he didn't suddenly burst into songs about the glory of moss.

Bohootus welcomed them to the Torallian Forest and pledged his people's support in their cause. But, before he could give them a tour of the sacred Mulch Temple of Gurrh, Zorell hissed.

Deanna thought that Zorell was just being rude to another mushroom, but she soon saw that his fur was standing up and his eyes were wide with fear. "He approaches," the cat hissed through bared teeth.

"Eldrack?" Deanna asked, pulling the wand out. Zorell nodded slightly, and Deanna asked Bohootus where they could go to hide from the dark wizard.

"Just ahead, there is a meadow," the great wizard said. "We can run into the meadow and ambush Eldrack when he enters. I have a plan that I am sure you will love."

"Fine," Deanna said. "Let's get moving." They all ran down the path, looking over their shoulders occasionally to see if Eldrack was behind them. He had not appeared by the time they reached a stand of bushes that Bohootus pointed to.

They were all able to hide behind the leafy bushes. Bohootus said that he would transform and put his plan into action.

"What do you mean transform?" Deanna asked.

"I am a great fan of the Mystical Guardians," Bohootus said proudly. "I have studied your world. I plan to transform into one of the most frightening animals from your world and scare Eldrack all the way out of the Torallian Forest."

"What animal?" Derek asked, but Bohootus was already running to a nearby bush and ducking down.

"Deanna," a deep voice boomed. "We really must talk. You know that your destiny lies with me."

Deanna wanted to stand up and send every spell she knew at Eldrack, but she stayed hidden and called back, "You lie, Eldrack, and I believe that you altered the prophecies in the Archive." She wasn't thinking about what she was saying. She just knew it was important to keep Eldrack distracted and give Bohootus time.

Derek, however, turned his head to look at her. He had not thought of the possibility of Eldrack changing the prophecies to trick them.

"Deanna, I would never be able to get past the traps that Gula Badu has set around the Archive." They could tell from the sound of his voice that he was moving around the meadow, but he did not seem to be getting closer to them. "Now, please come out. I promise that I only want to explain how we can help each other."

"I'm trying to think of things that I'd rather do than talk with you," Deanna said. "Swimming in jellybird goo comes to mind. Ooh, how about getting my head shaved by hair fairies while having Gong Beaters dribble slugfruit juice on me? Or, maybe a slap fight with Green Thumb?"

Eldrack was silent. Derek peeked out and thought that he saw the dark wizard laughing. "Very good, Deanna," Eldrack said, but he stopped. The bushes to his right rustled.

"That must be Bohootus," Deanna whispered. "I'll bet he turned himself into a lion."

Instead, a fat panda lumbered out from behind the bush and headed toward Eldrack. The plump creature raised a paw like it was going to hit

Eldrack, but then fell over and went to sleep."

"I expected something like this," Zorell said, looking at the ridiculous panda wizard snoring loudly at Eldrack's feet.

Deanna looked out and saw Eldrack holding his wand. One simple spell and their hiding place would be gone. They were in the middle of the meadow with no other shelter near them. She thought furiously. She would have to use defensive magic to stop Eldrack's attacks. She jumped out from behind the bush and held the wand out in front of her. Eldrack's first spell sent a wave of fiery light that crackled through the air. Deanna shouted *"Deflecto,"* but Eldrack's spell burned through her magical shield and knocked her backward.

"Slippero," Eldrack yelled. A river of oily liquid washed toward them. Deanna tried to use the *Umbrellius* spell to keep the slippery stuff off of them, but there was too much of it. She slipped and the Wand of Ondarell flew out of her hand. Derek lunged forward and caught the craggy stick that held so much power.

Tobungus and Zorell looked at Deanna trying to get up out of the slick goo. Then, they looked at Derek who had never had to face Eldrack in a magical duel yet. Derek felt their lack of confidence, but realized that he had studied defensive spells on the mornings when he got up early. With Deanna stuck in goo, he would have to try to block Eldrack's magic himself.

Eldrack's next spell was another wave of fiery light. Derek raised the wand and shouted *"Deflecto."* A shield of light appeared in front of Derek. He felt a wave of power as Eldrack's spell hit his shield. He was absorbing the power of Eldrack's spell. Derek's defensive spells were getting stronger, and he was blocking Eldrack's attacks easily.

Deanna finally got to her feet and was amazed at her brother's success with the wand. She noticed that he had a faint purple glimmer in his eyes. She still knew, however, that they had to find a way to escape from Eldrack, instead of just deflecting his attacks. She got an idea and reached into her backpack and took out a vial. As she put the vial to her lips, Tobungus cried, "No, not here."

"Don't worry, Tobungus," she said, "One drop of the chee chee bee honey will give me a power boost."

She drank the single drop and quickly understood why Tobungus had yelled at her. The honey's power caused the shrinking spell to wear off, and she grew to her normal size. She looked down and saw a toy-sized Eldrack looking up at her in fear. She picked him up and tossed him out of the miniature forest. "See, Tobungus. The honey helped me get rid of Eldrack."

"Just don't step on anybody I know," Tobungus said.

Deanna woke up Bohootus, the panda, and asked him to shrink her back down. After she was small again, they said their goodbyes, promising to visit the mushroom wizard on their way home. The group continued on their journey and reached the far edge of the Torallian Forest by nightfall.

5   What Rhymes with Dragon Breath?

The skies were darker than the twins were used to when they saw a sign saying that they were entering the Dragon Realm, the land of the Sky Dragons. The lights of Elestra's fifteen moons were much dimmer over the Dragon Realm because it was so far south, and the moons tended to orbit Elestra over the equator.

Deanna was still energized from the Chee Chee Bee Honey, and Derek was excited by his success against Eldrack, so they did not want to stop yet. The darkness reminded them of being back home in their backyard on a summer night. The winds were calm, and there was no sign of Eldrack. Tobungus was still beaming about showing his friends his home forest, and Zorell was happy to be away from so many mushroom people. Everyone was in good spirits and ready to continue their journey.

Suddenly, a jet of fire shot out from a mountainside far down the path. The group stopped in their tracks. After a few seconds, another blast followed the first. The twins were spellbound by the flames, and Deanna asked, "what was that?"

"That was just a dragon trying to sing a firesong," a deep whispering voice answered.

"What?" Deanna said, turning to see who had spoken. She and Derek had not seen the large green dragon come up behind them on the path.

The dragon said, "I'm sorry to have startled you, friends. I am usually rather clumsy, and most people hear me coming from two mountains away."

Deanna might have been frightened of an unknown dragon on a dark path at night, but one look at this dragon put her at ease. He had big, smiling eyes and a very long tongue that was dangling out the side of his mouth. She decided that he looked like a playful puppy, more than a scary dragon.

"My name's Deanna," she said. "And this is my brother, Derek." She pointed to Derek who was trying to figure out just how long the dragon was.

"It is good to meet you," the dragon said. "I am Togobogonogomogohogopogo, but my friends call me Shump."

"Okay, Shump," Deanna said. "What is a firesong?"

"Hmm?" Shump said. "Oh, yes, the dragon trying the firesong." He looked back to the distant mountain to where the jets of flame were still billowing. "A firesong is dragon poetry. A dragon comes up with something artistic to say and then says it with a series of fire spouts. The fiery display adds to the quality of the poem. To be honest, most dragons really stink at poetry. We just like to shoot fire around."

"I wonder what his poem is about," Derek said.

"Probably about getting rid of Olvard," Shump said.

"What do you mean 'getting rid of Olvard?'" Derek shot back in surprise. "Isn't Olvard the king?"

"Olvard's young," Shump said, shrugging his massive shoulders. "Some of the leaders of the Dragon Islands farther out have been looking for a chance to take over. Many dragons whisper about a rebellion against Olvard and the Old Order."

"Why do they want to get rid of Olvard?" Deanna asked.

"I don't think there's really a good reason," Shump answered. "My people support Olvard, and so do I. But, he's young, and he has not yet gone through the Ascension Ceremony, so many of the Outfliers think that he is weak and can be defeated easily."

"Who are the Outfliers?" Derek asked.

"The Outfliers are the leaders of the Dragon Islands on the far edges of the Dragon Realm. They call themselves the Outfliers because they fly in the areas outside of the main dragon kingdom."

"Wait a minute, Shump," Deanna said. "That dragon that's trying the firesong is further in, toward the heart of the Dragon Realm. I thought you said the Outfliers were on the edges of the realm."

"The Outfliers are gaining followers closer in," Shump said. "I think that Olvard has enemies within his castle, and I think those enemies are recruiting others."

"When will Olvard be ready to go through the Ascension Ceremony?" Derek asked.

"Olvard can do it anytime he chooses, but his advisers have told him that he must study more and build his strength so that he will be sure to pass the tests easily." Shump looked serious. "If Olvard does very well in the Ceremony, then the Outfliers will not dare try to overthrow him."

"That sounds reasonable," Deanna said. "I wish we could reach Olvard's castle tonight, so we don't lose any more time."

Before she knew it, Shump whipped his tail around, picked up all four travelers, and popped them on his back. His mighty wings flapped twice, and he was in the air, speeding toward a floating island with a huge castle at its center. He landed outside the castle's walls and used his tail to put the twins and their friends back on the ground. "Now, I must get home," Shump said. "My grandmother is making cupcakes, and I don't want to miss them."

"Oh, that's sweet," Deanna said. "What kind of cupcakes is she making?"

"Gravel!" Shump answered happily. "My favorite."

"Wow, that sounds yummy," Derek said. "We don't want to keep you from your cupcakes. Thanks for the ride."

"Anytime," Shump said, as he flew off toward a smaller floating island back in the direction they came from.

The gate to the castle was fifty feet high, and hundreds of torches lined the castle's outer walls. "What do we do now?" Derek asked, looking toward Deanna.

"We knock," Tobungus said. He pushed his way past the twins and used a metal knocker to announce their arrival.

The huge gate slowly rose from the ground. It creaked and moaned under its own weight. Finally, it was high enough for them to enter. They slowly walked into the castle and found an old-looking olive green dragon with patches of maroon scales waiting for them. The dragon was hunched over, and had a beard of white whiskers on his chin.

"Welcome to Olvard's castle," the ancient dragon said. "How can I help you?"

"We need to speak with Olvard about our mission from King Barado," Derek blurted out.

"What?" the dragon said.

Derek repeated what he had said.

"What?" the dragon said again.

Derek repeated himself again, and again, the dragon said, "What?"

"Maybe he's deaf," Deanna whispered to Derek.

"I'm not deaf," the dragon screeched.

"Okay, then," Derek said, "we need to speak with Olvard."

"What?" the dragon said again.

Derek was about to get angry with the dragon, when another voice cut in, "Uncle, leave our visitors alone." The twins looked over and saw the young green dragon that they had met at the picnic coming down a massive staircase.

"Hello, children," the green dragon said, "we meet again."

"Olvard," Deanna said, "are we glad to see

you!"

"Well, I'm glad to see you too," Olvard replied. "And, I'm sorry about my uncle. He's just trying to tease you a little bit. He doesn't get out much anymore, and he gets playful."

"No problem," Derek said. "Look, we don't mean to be rude, but we have come to your kingdom to find a moonstone so that we can stop Eldrack from taking over Elestra."

"That's certainly an important quest," Olvard said. "The problem is that I don't know where any moonstone is in the kingdom. Perhaps I can give you a tour of the kingdom tomorrow and we can search for the moonstone together."

"That would be wonderful," Deanna said. "I hope you don't mind, but we need to get some sleep before we continue our search."

"Of course," Olvard said, "I can show you to a room for the night. It has a dragon bed in it, so there will be plenty of room for everyone. I'll have one of the cooks send some snacks to your room."

When they got to the room, they were amazed at what they saw. The bed was sixty feet long and forty feet wide. Almost immediately, there was a knock on the door. A small, blue dragon was waiting outside with a cart that had sandwiches, fruit, and pitchers of water and juice.

They thanked the dragon cook and sat down for a late night snack.

Once they had finished their sandwiches, everyone headed to the giant bed. The pillows were the size garden sheds. The bed was surprisingly soft, and they all fell asleep immediately.

In the morning, they wandered out and found Olvard eating toast and drinking tea from a trough in one of the castle's gardens. "Ah, my friends," Olvard said when he saw them. "Join me for breakfast. Eat and then we can get going."

Derek and Deanna shared a piece of toast the size of a billboard. Actually, they each broke off a piece the size of a normal slice of toast. Tobungus ate berries that he had hidden in one of his pockets, and Zorell licked crumbs and butter off of the toast.

When everyone was full, Olvard led the group through the halls of the castle to start the tour of his kingdom. He pointed to paintings of past Dragon Kings, and made comments about each one. Telgaar's painting seemed to be the biggest, and the twins assumed it was because he was the last Red Dragon.

Derek asked Olvard about one painting that seemed a bit strange. In it, the dragon king was facing away from the artist. The picture was of his back.

"Ah, yes, that is Goomard," Olvard explained. "He believed that he was the fastest dragon ever, and he loved to race other dragons as much as possible. He said that his painting should be of his back since that was the only view that all of the dragons who raced him had. He figured that people would recognize his back more easily than his face, since they always saw it when he beat them in a race."

"Wow," Derek said, "He must have been really fast."

"No, not really," Olvard said. "Sure he was good at beating cows in races, but any dragon could beat him. He always had some crazy excuse about why the race didn't count: he got tripped by a cloud, his crown was too heavy, wing cramp, and so on."

After they had seen all of the paintings of past Dragon Kings, Olvard led them out of the castle, and through the town that surrounded it. He told them that he would show them all of the most important places in his kingdom, so that they could get clues about where to search for the moonstone. Their first stop was a bench in a grassy park. "This is where I caught my pet spider bird," Olvard said. "It is a very special place for me."

He took them to a series of odd locations.

There was the puddle where he thought his foot sank, the tree that he mistakenly burned down while reciting a firesong for Mother's Day, a lake where he had had a staring contest with himself in the water's reflection, and a farm that grew the best hay in the whole kingdom.

"Maybe we should try to learn more about what was going on a long time ago in the kingdom," Deanna said gently. "The moonstone was probably hidden in the kingdom two or three hundred years ago."

"Well, then, we should go to the Hall of Red Kings where you can learn about our heroic Red Dragon kings and the history of the Dragon Realms," Olvard said. He guided them to a massive stone building with pillars that reached to the sky.

"Olvard, I have a silly question," Deanna asked. The young king looked at her. "Sometimes people say Dragon Realm and sometimes they say Dragon Realms. Why do they do that?"

"The Sky Dragons used to be divided into many small kingdoms or realms," Olvard explained. "Everyone got used to saying Dragon Realms. When all of the dragon communities were united, they became the Dragon Realm. Today, Dragon Realm and Dragon Realms mean the same thing . . . to most dragons."

They toured the museum with Olvard, and read about the past Red Dragons. Deanna stopped in front of an exhibit about Telgaar, the last Red Dragon. "Olvard," she said, "I still don't understand how a dragon turns red."

"No one knows for sure," Olvard explained. "Each Dragon King must prepare for years. When he is ready, the new king flies into the pit of Mt. Infernus to face a great challenge. He must use his intelligence, strength, and bravery."

Olvard looked nervous, but continued, "Telgaar never told anyone what he had to do to become a Red Dragon, but he did say that intelligence, strength, and bravery all come together and become one thing, and when a king understands that, he can become a Red Dragon."

Derek and Deanna stood before a huge painting of Telgaar and were mesmerized by the power in his eyes. Olvard interrupted their thoughts. "I feel lucky that you came to visit." Derek looked confused. "Before Telgaar went through his Ascension Ceremony, a Mystical Guardian, Barndoble, came to visit the kingdom. Telgaar must have felt like the Guardian's presence was a sign that he was ready for the Ceremony. Perhaps your visit today is a sign that I am getting close to being ready." He lowered his head and walked on to the next painting.

They continued to walk around the museum for another hour, and then decided to go back to the castle for lunch. As soon as they left the building, three large green dragons came toward them from the main road. "Olvard," the largest one said. "You're supposed to be back at the castle studying."

"Oh, no," Olvard said sheepishly.

6 The Enemy Within

Olvard stood looking at the three huge green dragons that stood before him. They had just told him that he should be at the castle studying for his Ascension Ceremony, instead of running around with friends. "Yes, I know, Bronn," Olvard said, looking embarrassed.

"You'll never be ready for the Ceremony if you don't get serious," the second green dragon said.

"But, I was showing my friends around the kingdom," Olvard replied.

"There is danger all around, Olvard," the dragon named Bronn said. "You must study and work to get strong enough to stop the Outfliers."

"But, I'm ready now," Olvard said.

"Ready now?" the second dragon repeated, holding back a laugh. "If you go into the volcano now, you'll be a black dragon, as in black like a piece of charcoal. Why don't you just listen to us? You may never be ready to tame the heart of Mt. Infernus. We know better than you."

The other dragons stomped away, leaving Olvard feeling embarrassed in front of the twins.

"It's okay," Deanna said. "We know that you're ready for the ceremony."

"How could you know?" Olvard said under his breath. "They're right. I'm a failure. I'll never become a red dragon."

"Why is it so important to become a red dragon?" Derek asked. "I mean, there haven't been many red dragons. Weren't any of the other kings strong leaders?"

"You don't understand," Olvard shot back. "If I want to be the king who saves the Dragon Realms from the Outfliers, I have to be a red dragon."

Derek didn't know what else to say. He turned to ask Tobungus and Zorell what they thought, hoping they would know what to say to cheer the young dragon up. He was surprised to see Zorell looking at Tobungus, staring really, without his usual look of irritation. Zorell was looking at the mushroom man as if something very serious had just happened.

Tobungus did not return his look. Instead, he was watching Bronn and the other dragons who were walking away. His look was dark, and his eyes seemed to hide something elusive.

"What's wrong, Tobungus?" Derek asked.

Very slowly, Tobungus turned to Derek and said, "We have to watch out for those dragons." He cocked his head toward Zorell and added, "This would be a good time to use that cat hearing of yours."

"I'm on it," Zorell replied, before running off down the path after the dragons. He stayed in the long grass, out of sight.

"What's going on?" Derek asked Tobungus. "I've never seen you and Zorell speak to each other like that. You're usually both trying to come up with the ultimate insult to sling at each other, and now you act like you're allies."

"There are times, Derek, when even Zorell and I can put our differences aside in the cause that drives your quest," Tobungus said. Zorell knows that my people have a unique ability to sense feelings in dragons. Those dragons are hiding a dark secret, but I don't know what it is. Zorell and I have used a truce spell which will make us work together in peace. I have to warn you, though. After the spell wears off, we'll be worse than ever."

Tobungus took out a small notebook and wrote something in it, and then hurried off down the path after Zorell.

Olvard cut in, "Look, I know that Bronn's not

the nicest dragon you'll ever meet, but my family has always trusted him."

Deanna joined the conversation. "I don't mean to sound rude, but the only member of your family we've met is your uncle, and he seems like he'd trust anyone."

"My uncle is a great dragon," Olvard shot back.

"I'm sure he is," Deanna said, "But, well, I guess what I'm trying to ask is if Bronn served other kings."

"Of course, he has," Olvard answered. "My uncle has trusted him since the last days of his reign."

"Your uncle was a king?" Deanna said in surprise.

Olvard looked at Deanna with a mix of confusion and irritation. "My uncle is Telgaar, the last great Red Dragon."

"What happened to him?" Derek asked. "I mean . . . he's not red anymore," he added quickly.

"Most Dragon Kings give up their thrones when they get too old," Olvard explained. "Then, they spend the rest of their lives learning to swim."

"Learning to swim?" Deanna said in disbelief.

"I know that might sound strange to you, but

dragons don't usually swim because the water isn't good for their fire," Olvard replied. "Learning to swim is a sign of great courage. The only thing more feared than water to a dragon is ice."

"But why is he green?" Derek asked again.

"I'm not sure," Olvard said nervously. "He seems to have forgotten a lot of what happened at the end of his reign. He was in a lot of battles, so we all assumed that he had just used up his power."

"Is that possible?" Deanna asked.

"I don't know," Olvard said.

"Okay, then," Deanna said, "since he was the last Red Dragon, can't he help you learn what to do in the ceremony?"

"No," Olvard said quietly. "He doesn't remember anything about that time."

"I wonder if someone could have used a spell on him," Derek said in a voice just above a whisper.

"Well, if you're thinking that Bronn used magic on Telgaar, you're wrong," Olvard said. "Dragon wizards are purple. They can't hide their color, so I know that Bronn does not use magic, at least not magic strong enough to steal the power of a Red Dragon."

Deanna wanted to say something, but she didn't want to start an argument.

Olvard looked like he was getting upset.

"Look, I've got to get back to studying for the ceremony." He was about to head back to the castle.

"Wait a second," Deanna said sternly. She was beginning to think that Olvard liked to have people boss him around. "We can't wait any longer to find the moonstone. Where could a moonstone be hidden that would make it hard for a dark wizard to find?"

"I suppose if you're clever enough, you could hide a moonstone anywhere," Olvard said. "But, any of the fire-spots would be good places because they are too hot for anyone other than dragons."

"What are the fire-spots?" Deanna asked.

"The fire springs and volcanoes around the Dragon Realm are known as the fire-spots. Only dragons can withstand the heat in those places."

"If dragons can go to the fire-spots, I don't think the moonstone could be there. It has to be someplace that would be hidden from most people and dragons," Deanna said, thinking out loud.

"The only place that is truly isolated in the Dragon Realm is Mt. Infernus," Olvard said.

"Isn't that where the Dragon Kings go for their Ascension Ceremonies?" Derek asked.

"Yes," Olvard said. "And I should be preparing so that I will be ready when my time comes."

"I'm sorry," Deanna said. "We're all sorry that we got you in trouble. You can get back to the castle. Would you mind if we looked around some more?"

"That will be fine," Olvard said. "My people are friendly to visitors, so you should be safe in my kingdom. When you have finished your search for the day, you are welcome to come back to the castle for dinner."

Derek and Deanna thanked Olvard and sat down on the steps of the museum, as the young dragon king took flight toward his castle. Deanna pulled the necklace off of her neck and opened the charm. The Book of Spells popped out of the charm and grew into a full sized book.

"What are you doing?" Derek asked Deanna.

"I started thinking about a good hiding place for the moonstone," Deanna began. "It had to be hidden by one of our ancestors, right?" Derek nodded. "Well, a human wizard would want to hide the moonstone where people, or dragons, couldn't easily find it. Mt. Infernus seems like a good spot."

"But, Deanna," Derek said, "Even dragons stay away from Mt. Infernus. Only the kings who prepare for years can survive there."

Derek thought for a moment, then exclaimed, "Wait a minute, Deanna! You may be right. Olvard told us that a Mystical Guardian came to the Dragon Realms just before Telgaar went through his ceremony. Maybe that's when the moonstone was hidden and maybe Telgaar became red because he did something heroic to help the Guardian hide the stone."

"Right," Deanna said. "That's what I think too. That made me think about a chapter of spells that deals with heat. When I first read about them, I thought they would be spells that let the wizard use heat as a weapon, but they're not. They're spells that protect the wizard against heat. We don't know who wrote the Book of Spells. Maybe, the Mystical Guardians wrote the book as they learned more magic and passed it down through the generations."

"I see," Derek said. "They would have put the spells in the book for a reason. Maybe they put the heat protection spells in so that future Guardians could go into the volcano and get the moonstone back."

"We've got to go to Mt. Infernus," Deanna nearly shouted. "But first, we've got to tell Olvard what we figured out."

"We've also got to find Tobungus and

Zorell," Derek said.

"They can work together while we're in the volcano," Deanna replied. "It will be good for them."

They hurried back to the castle and found Olvard in a large room, reading massive books on dragon history. He looked miserable.

"What's wrong?" Deanna asked the dragon king.

"Bronn's already been in here to yell at me about falling behind in my studies," Olvard answered. "I'm afraid that I have to get back to work now."

"But, Olvard," Derek said, "We think that the moonstone is in Mt. Infernus. We have to go to the volcano now."

"I would not advise you to do that," Olvard said. "Your people cannot survive in the volcano. You must search elsewhere."

"Olvard, the moonstone's there. The Mystical Guardian came before Telgaar's Ascension Ceremony, and we think that's when he hid the moonstone in the volcano," Deanna explained.

"Yeah, Olvard," Derek said. "Telgaar probably went into the volcano to help the Guardian."

"Children," Olvard said, "When Dragon

Kings are little, they are taught that they must work hard to become red. We all want to be the most powerful king ever. We all want to be red. Telgaar would not have gone into the volcano unless he was ready for the Ceremony. Now, I just have to figure out what he learned." He saw that they were going to continue arguing with him. "Really, I must get back to my studies."

"Fine," Deanna said. "We're going to Mt. Infernus. We'll see you when we have the moonstone in our hands."

"Okay, goodbye then," Olvard said, with his nose already buried in another book.

"Come on, Deanna," Derek said.

Derek and Deanna rushed out of the castle and headed toward Mt. Infernus. Deanna was already going over the spells she would use, and Derek was thinking about the best way to use the magical socks and chee chee bee honey.

In their excitement over figuring out where the moonstone must be hidden, they had forgotten to find out where Tobungus and Zorell were. They did not know that their friends were hiding behind a fountain on the far side of the castle listening to a very interesting conversation.

7 The Rise of the King

Tobungus and Zorell stayed hidden until Bronn and the others left the courtyard where they were having their secret meeting. "We have to warn Olvard," Zorell said.

"We also need to find Derek and Deanna," Tobungus added.

"Maybe they're with Olvard," Zorell suggested as they charged up the stairs to the castle's back entrance. They snuck through the halls to avoid other dragons and found Olvard in his study, still reading the books on dragon history.

"Olvard," Zorell called out as they entered the room.

"Yes, my friends," Olvard said. "I don't mean to be rude, but I really must continue my studies."

"Why? Because Bronn told you to?" Tobungus asked.

"As a matter of fact, yes," Olvard said.

"Olvard, we just heard Bronn talking with your other advisors. They're working with the Outfliers. They're trying to keep you from the

Ascension Ceremony so that you won't gain power. They want to take over and get rid of you," Zorell said. "They're planning to join Eldrack."

"I don't believe you," Olvard said. "I've already spoken with the children about Bronn. I don't think you have gotten to know him well enough yet."

"Speaking of Deanna and Derek," Tobungus said, "Where are they?"

"Hmm?" Olvard asked, surprised by the sudden change in topic. "Oh yes. They said something about figuring out that the moonstone was in Mt. Infernus. They left about an hour ago."

"What do you mean in Mt. Infernus?" Zorell asked. "Don't you mean 'on' Mt. Infernus?"

"No, I mean in," Olvard replied. "They think it's in the volcano."

"We have to go to them," Zorell said hurriedly.

"Well, off you go, then," Olvard said, impatient to get back to his studies.

"You have to come with us," Tobungus said.

"No, I can't," Olvard murmured. "I'm not ready yet." He buried his nose in his book again.

Tobungus and Zorell both saw that it would be useless to try to convince Olvard to come with them. They hurried out of the castle and looked down the path that led to Mt. Infernus. Derek and Deanna were nowhere to be seen. They realized that the twins must be nearing the volcano.

"Do you have any of that chee chee bee honey?" Zorell asked.

"Yep," Tobungus said. "I saved some for myself. I see where you're going with this, but even with the honey, I'll never be fast enough to catch up with them..."

Zorell looked discouraged.

As Tobungus reached into his shoe bag, he added, "... But, you will."

* *

The twins were nearing the summit of Mt. Infernus and would soon enter the volcanic crater. Derek turned around as he heard a rumbling down the path. To his surprise, he saw Zorell running like a cheetah towing a rope pulling Tobungus on roller skates.

"Woohoo," Tobungus yelled as the wind whipped around him. Within seconds, Zorell had reached Derek and Deanna, and Tobungus used the toe brakes on his skates and did an extra little spin move as he stopped.

"Where have you guys been?" Derek asked

Zorell.

"We were following Bronn and the other advisers," the cat replied. "And, we found out why Tobungus sensed something secretive and dark about Bronn."

The twins looked anxious to hear what they had learned. "Bronn is working with the Outfliers."

Derek nodded, as if he suspected that Bronn was up to no good. Before he could say anything, Tobungus added, "And, the worst part is that we think that the Outfliers are allied with Eldrack."

"Another piece of the puzzle," Deanna said. "What did they say about Eldrack?"

"They were talking about the magical help that they had gotten," Tobungus said.

"And how happy they were that it was finally paying off," Zorell added.

"Magical help?" Deanna murmured to herself.

"I'll bet they've been planning this for a long time," Derek said. He saw the others looking at him expectantly. "Okay, Olvard said that Telgaar trusted Bronn in the last years of his reign. Something happened to Telgaar to make him lose his power. Now, Bronn says that the magical plan is finally paying off."

"Yes, but if they stole Telgaar's power almost

two hundred years ago, why didn't they take over then?" Tobungus mused.

"Because Eldrack was not ready to face King Barado then," Deanna said. "If Eldrack is behind this plot, then he would have told Bronn when he and the Outfliers could take over. He would have wanted the dragons to wait until he got close to capturing the fifteenth generation of our family or until he had the moonstones. He probably told Bronn to make sure that the young king remains weak. So, Bronn keeps Olvard from going through the ceremony and convinces him that he is powerless. They can take over easily and join Eldrack."

"That makes a lot of sense," Zorell said. "We should hurry." He purred as he thought. "But, how are we going to go into the volcano?"

"First, we need to put on some socks," Derek said.

He pulled out the dirty, old socks worn by the ice wizard Glorat and handed everyone a pair. Tobungus pulled the socks all the way up his short, stocky legs, and Zorell looked ridiculous with the socks bunched up over his paws.

"Next, we'll need some chee chee bee honey," Derek added. He gave everyone a drop. "Now, it's up to Deanna."

Deanna pulled out Wand of Ondarell and pointed it upward. *"Infernius protecto,"* she shouted. A golden shield glowed all around them. She picked up some sand from the path and pointed the wand at it. *"Wrappus shieldus,"* she said and threw the sand above Derek. When the sand hit the shield, part of the golden curtain fell around Derek and wrapped him in its glow. She repeated this spell for Zorell, Tobungus, and herself. They were all coated in a heat shield that she hoped would protect them inside Elestra's hottest volcano.

They scaled the rest of the path to the rim of the volcano's crater. When they reached the top, they saw that areas around the edges had hardened into smooth chutes that could be used like slides to get into the heart of the volcano. "I'll go first," Deanna said bravely, holding the wand in front of her. The others understood that she would be ready to use other spells if they needed more protection. She took a deep breath and hopped onto the slide and slid deep into Mt. Infernus.

Deanna shot out of the bottom of the slide onto a round rocky island in the middle of a lake of magma. Derek, Zorell, and finally Tobungus joined her on the solid platform.

On the far side of the bubbling lake, they saw a large island with a temple made of the blackest stone they had ever seen. There was a series of small stones jutting out of the magma from their location all the way to the temple.

"Well, this should be fun," Derek said. "I guess I'll go first this time."

Tobungus gulped, and Zorell secretly wished that he and Tobungus had not caught up with the twins. Derek stepped onto the first stone and wobbled back and forth. He caught his balance, and moved onto the next one. Deanna followed him, and then Tobungus went next. When the first three reached the large island, they turned to see Zorell still standing on the first platform.

"Come on, Zorell," Tobungus called. Without warning, the cat ran and jumped from one stone to the next. He was across the lake in seconds.

"I just wanted to be sure that you were all off of the stones," Zorell purred. "Now, about this moonstone."

Deanna and Derek walked next to each other as they approached the Temple's arched entrance. On either side of the opening stood a giant crystal statue of a guard with a sword pointing up toward the top of the volcano. The guards were as clear as glass and seemed to glow against the brilliant black walls of the Temple. The only color on the statues were tattoos of red dragons on their right arms.

Derek took a step to enter the Temple when the guard statue on his right turned and said, "Who comes to the Heart of Magma Temple?"

"Um, I'm Derek," the young wizard replied.

"Okay, just checking," the guard said and returned to his original position.

Derek walked in and Deanna followed. The guard turned to her and said, "Who comes to the Heart of Magma Temple?"

"My name's Deanna," she replied.

"That's a pretty name," the guard said. "Listen, someone named Derek passed through here a while ago. If you see him, say hi for me."

"Sure," Deanna said. "And, in a few seconds, two more visitors will enter the temple. Their names are Tobungus and Zorell."

"Busy day," the guard muttered. "May I ask why you have come here?"

Deanna wondered whether she should tell the guard that they were looking for the moonstone, but decided that the Mystical Guardian who had put the moonstone in the Temple probably told the guards to work with future Guardians. "We are searching for a moonstone, and we believe that it is here in the Heart of Magma Temple."

"Very well," the guard said. "I wish you luck, and I would advise you to stay warm."

Deanna looked puzzled by this advice. "I don't think we'll have any trouble staying warm in the pit of a volcano."

"You've been warned," the guard said.

When they had all entered the Temple, they saw a maze of fireballs, miniature volcanic cones rising from the floor, and magma dripping from the ceiling. On the far side of the Temple stood another crystal guard. This one was much larger than the others. His sword was the size of a tree and it seemed to feed the fire inside the temple. It pulsed a deep red-orange. It was the only part of the statue that was not clear, except for the tattoo of the red dragon on his massive right arm. Even from this great distance, Deanna thought that she saw one of the eyes of the dragon in the tattoo shimmer with a blue light.

"There it is," Deanna shouted. "The moonstone's in the dragon tattoo's eye."

"This ought to be fun," Derek said, as he took a deep breath and began crossing the fiery hall within the temple.

* *

Olvard was taking notes on what he was reading. He had just written, "Every young dragon king wants to grow up to be a red dragon." He flipped back through his notes and realized that he had written the same thing many times before. He thought back to his childhood. He had always been told that he should work hard to become a red dragon. But why? Red Dragons were the most powerful kings. *Everyone wanted to be the most powerful king*, he thought.

His thoughts drifted to Telgaar. What had he figured out before his Ascension Ceremony? Telgaar did not seem like the most powerful dragon, even in the paintings from his days as a Red Dragon. *Oh, to be like Telgaar*, Olvard thought.

"Wait a second," he muttered to himself. "Telgaar is not great because he was red. He is great because he united the kingdom and kept peace."

He thought furiously. His kingdom was in danger. His first thought was of his kingdom, not of himself. He realized that the kingdom was more important than the king. Then, he understood what Telgaar had learned. It didn't matter how much strength, intelligence, or bravery a king had. It only mattered how he used those things.

Olvard pushed the stacks of books onto the floor and rose up out of his seat. He headed toward the door to look for Bronn.

As Olvard walked the halls of the castle, he grew angrier at Bronn's treachery. He felt like he was growing larger and braver with each step. Up ahead, he saw the massive doors to his Meeting Chambers. No doubt, Bronn would be there making plans with the allies of the Outfliers.

Olvard rose up and threw the doors open with a mighty push. The wooden doors were fifty feet tall and made a crashing sound that echoed throughout the castle.

"Olvard," Bronn said in surprise. "Why aren't you studying?"

"You'd like that, wouldn't you?" Olvard shot back.

"Of course, I would," Bronn said. "Every time you stop to play, you make it harder for yourself. I've told you time and again that you have to work harder if you want to succeed in your ceremony."

"You don't care about my ceremony," Olvard said. "You want to keep me weak."

"How dare you," Bronn said. "I am your faithful advisor, but you are right that you are weak. I am here to make you strong."

"No," Olvard bellowed. "I was weak. You did make me strong, but only by accident. When I realized that you wanted to take power in my kingdom and join with the forces of darkness, I learned what I need to know to succeed."

"I'm sorry, Your Highness," Bronn said, motioning to his fellow advisors. "I must insist that you stay in the castle and listen to me."

Olvard rose up and flapped his wings to lift off from the ground. He turned toward the back of the room.

"I see that you're running away," Bronn said. "And you said you were strong. You'll never change. You'll always be weak."

To Bronn's surprise, Olvard continued to rise. He was not heading toward the doors at the back of the room, but instead was heading for the huge red glass windows near the ceiling.

"It is time," Olvard said before crashing through the windows and heading for Mt. Infernus.

8 Out of the Frying Pan and into the Fire

Inside the Temple, Derek and Deanna reached a small lake of magma which was too large to jump. "Alright, everyone," Deanna said, "Stick close together. I'm going to use a Levitation Spell." She held the wand out and muttered the words, "*Levitato ovallo.*" A shimmering egg shaped bubble rose up with the twins and their two friends inside. Deanna waved her wand toward the statue, and they began floating over the pool of magma.

The heat from the magma was blistering, and quickly made the group bounce around as the spell weakened. Deanna shouted the words to a heat shield spell which strengthened their bubble. The heat was too much, and soon the shield began to glow a bright orange, as if it were about to catch fire.

Deanna used another heat shield spell, but as she did, she had to stop guiding the bubble toward the statue. They were sitting motionless above the middle of the magma pool.

"What are we going to do?" Derek asked worriedly.

"I'm working on it," Deanna said. She knew that each heat shield spell was weakening more quickly as the heat grew stronger.

Before she could think up another spell, she heard a whooshing noise from above. In the distance, she saw Olvard swooping into the Temple. Her hope was quickly dashed, however, as she saw a group of six or seven large dragons following him, shooting jets of fire after him.

Derek and Deanna were expecting Olvard to look scared, and even to ask for their help against his attackers. But, as he got closer, they saw that there was something different about him. He had grown, and he looked confident. He was faster than his pursuers, and he was able to fly between geysers of magma and columns of hardened volcanic rock.

Olvard swooped down and picked the group up just as the bubble was ready to burst. "How can I help?" he asked.

"We have to get to that statue over there," Derek said. "The moonstone's in the arm."

"You got it," Olvard said, looking over his shoulder.

Deanna wondered what Olvard was looking back at. When she turned around, she saw that he had been hit with several jets of fire from the other dragons. His tail and left leg were injured, but he continued to fly on as if nothing had happened.

Deanna raised the wand and shot beams of ice at the other dragons, which made them temporarily veer off from their attack.

They were only seconds away from the statue, and they could see that the fire seemed to pulse from the guard's sword. As Olvard curved around the statue, Tobungus seized the moment and pulled out a lasso. He shouted to Deanna, "You need to free the moonstone, and I'll grab it with my lasso."

Deanna thought about one spell that seemed odd, until she realized that she needed to use magic to remove magic. "*Eliminatus magicarium,*" she yelled over the sounds of Olvard's flapping wings, the sizzling attacks, and the churning magma. A quick bolt of energy hit the moonstone which began to shake loose from the statue's arm.

Tobungus swung the rope around the moonstone and flung it toward Zorell who batted the shimmering blue stone to Deanna. She grabbed it and shoved it into her pocket.

Almost immediately, the guard's sword changed from orange to blue and instead of fire, it shot ice around the Temple.

"That should cool things down," Derek said.

"Something's not right," Deanna called out.

As the air cooled around them, the heat shield she was using to protect them was weakening more quickly. Olvard seemed to be slowing down.

"Look," Derek said, pointing at the other dragons. They were speeding up and were not being affected by the strange icy magic. He noticed that the dragons were wearing white amulets which gave off an icy light. "Eldrack must have given them those things to protect themselves," he shouted.

"All of our spells only work here if it's hot," Deanna said. "And, it looks like Olvard needs the heat."

"We need to get to the far side of the Temple," Derek said, pointing to an area that looked like a cauldron of boiling lava. He scooted up Olvard's neck and yelled, "Olvard, try to get over there to the right. It should be hotter over there. We can fight back."

"I'll do my best," Olvard panted. He flapped his wings with everything he had. The attacks from the other dragons were clearly hurting him, and the cool air was weakening him even further. He struggled against the cold that was stealing his strength. Finally, he reached the bowl-shaped lake of magma.

"Deanna," Derek said, "You have to make

your strongest heat shield yet. Olvard has to go down by the lava to get his strength back, so we have to hold out until he regains his power."

"I'll try," Deanna said. She closed her eyes. Now that they were close to the lava, she was able to draw on the heat and create a new heat shield which was stronger than her earlier attempts. As Olvard lowered toward the magma, one of the dragons hit him with a shocking jolt, and the bubble carrying the twins and their friends slipped off of his back.

Deanna worked to keep them hovering over the magma, as Olvard began to rise further away from the bubbling lake.

"What's going on?" Derek called. He quickly realized that the other dragons were using magic to keep Olvard away from the heat he needed.

"Well, it looks like we'll all be part of a big bowl of lava soup," Tobungus said.

"It would be funny, if it weren't so frightening," Zorell added. "It really does look like a giant soup pot."

"Soup," Derek muttered, almost involuntarily. He began to twitch. "Soup, soup, soup," he chanted as his nose began to itch. "Tobungus, get your lasso ready."

"Huh?" Tobungus said.

"Swing it around that pillar of rock on the wall over there." Tobungus saw the piece of rock jutting out and wrapped his lasso around it.

Derek turned to Deanna and said, "Make sure that everyone stays together in the bubble." Before Deanna could ask what he was planning, he looked down at the magma and said, "That's one . . . big . . . pot . . . of soup!"

Derek felt like he was about to sneeze. He kept looking at the magma soup. He felt Rorrdoogo's soup allergy welling up inside him. He could no longer control it. He let out a sneeze that sounded like it was the combined sneezes of both wooden giants standing outside the Atteelian Orchard. The shock wave went straight down and hit the surface of the magma. Deanna swung the bubble away from the cauldron just as a column of lava shot up and engulfed Olvard who fell into the cauldron.

"Oh, no," Deanna screamed. "Olvard!"

Bronn swooped in and said, "Now you see that Olvard was weak. We will unite the kingdom and move in a new direction. We will restore glory to the Dragon Realms."

"Not so fast," came a deep bellowing voice. The chamber began to rumble, and the magma began to bubble. Bronn turned around to see a massive red dragon emerging from the magma.

"Olvard?" Bronn whispered. "A red dragon? Impossible!"

"I told you that you made me strong," Olvard said.

"Not strong enough," Bronn roared. Recovering from his surprise at Olvard's transformation, he reached for the amulet around his neck.

But Bronn had forgotten about Deanna. She raised her wand and shot a bolt of lightning at the amulet, blowing it into dust. She quickly blew the amulets off of Bronn's allies, who now faced Olvard without the magic that Deanna was sure Eldrack had given them.

Olvard rose into the air and swooped around the others. He used his tail to knock them toward the icy side of the Temple, where they froze, looking like dragon statues, next to the guard statue.

When Olvard landed back by the twins, he said, "They can stay here, in this icy prison, until we figure out how to deal with them."

He picked up Derek, Deanna, Tobungus, and Zorell, and headed out of the Temple and toward the mouth of the volcano. "Wait," he said, swinging back around and picking up the frozen Bronn, "We may need to find out who else was helping him."

A crowd of dragons had gathered around Mt. Infernus. Every dragon in the kingdom had heard that Olvard had run away from the castle and Bronn had followed him. Some were whispering that Bronn would finally take over and send Olvard away.

The crowds heard a rumbling. They held their breath, waiting to see who would emerge. To their surprise, a huge red dragon flew out of the volcano and hovered in front of the masses.

"Eldrack's followers have been vanquished," Olvard boomed. "Now, we must unite to make the Dragon Realms greater than they have ever been."

The dragons who had gathered were amazed that they had a new red dragon, and that Olvard had been the one to transform into the next red dragon. He sounded so strong and so sure of himself. It started slowly, but before long, the crowd was chanting, "Olvard, Olvard!" to the young dragon who had really just become a king.

Olvard shot a huge jet of flames straight up and lit the sky for miles around. Dragons who had not known about his transformation saw the fiery blast and flew to join the crowd. The chants of Olvard's name grew louder as the crowd swelled.

Finally, Olvard raised his hand and said,

"Fellow dragons, I thank you for joining me here. We have much work to do to save the Dragon Realm and stop the Outfliers. Go now and gather your brothers, your sisters, and your friends. We will fly together to face our enemies."

The dragons cheered their leader and took to the skies. The sounds of flapping wings and the light and heat from hundreds of jets of fire transformed the calm, dark night into a party to celebrate the new king.

9 Return of the King

Olvard flew into the courtyard of the castle and landed near a fountain. Derek and Deanna slid down onto the ground, with Tobungus and Zorell right behind them. As Olvard set Bronn down, Deanna looked sideways at Derek.

"What?" he asked, looking back.

"What kind of magic did you use back there?" she asked.

"What do you mean?" Derek replied. Then he realized what she meant. "That wasn't really magic."

"It looked like magic to me," Deanna said.

"Nope, just an allergy to soup," Derek replied. "Rorrdoogo said that the allergy would become a super-allergy for a while before it wore off. Just hearing Tobungus say that the lava cauldron looked like soup was enough to set it off."

"So, maybe it wasn't your magic," she said, "but you figured out what to do, so you still saved us all."

Derek cocked his head a bit and thought about what his sister said. It was nice to feel like he had saved them after all of the times that Deanna had used her magic to save the day. He had used a spell to freeze Eldrack when they were under Tarook's Temple, but this time, Derek felt like he did much more.

Deanna was startled by Olvard gently tapping her on the shoulder. "Pardon me," he said, "but I may need your help in thawing Bronn out."

"Sure," Deanna said, raising the Wand of Ondarell. "But, I don't think we should thaw him all the way. We don't want him to escape."

"Good idea," Olvard said.

Deanna waved a weak stream of fire over Bronn and watched as some of the ice covering him began to melt and run onto the courtyard stones. Within minutes, the traitor Bronn was shivering, but ice still covered his wings and legs so he was unable to fly or run away.

"Now, Bronn," Olvard said in an almost hissing voice, "you will tell us who else is working with the Outfliers."

Bronn wanted to resist, but the cold was too much, and he said, "The Cascadian Barons and their armies are the main leaders of the Outfliers. They were going to be the army of our new kingdom."

"We will deal with them," Olvard hissed, but I have one other question. "What have you done to

Telgaar?"

"In my office, you will find a glowing green vial," Bronn said through chattering teeth. "It contains Telgaar's power."

"Thank you," Olvard said sincerely.

"Are you going to freeze him again?" Tobungus asked, clearly nervous about the dragon who led the attack that almost landed him in a sea of magma.

"No, my friend," Olvard said. "The kingdom must heal. Bronn will answer for his crimes, but we must be true to what we believe. If I want other dragons to respect me and to treat me fairly, then I must treat them fairly. Every one of them. I will not punish Bronn out of anger. I will allow the laws of the Realm to handle him."

Olvard turned to Bronn and breathed a soft jet of fire on the frozen dragon, thawing him completely.

"Thank you, King Olvard," Bronn said humbly. "I was wrong to doubt your power. I thought that I knew the right path for the kingdom, and I believed what some other people said. I have no one to blame but myself."

"Yes, well, we will have plenty of time to discuss what you have done," Olvard said. "For now, you will have to be confined to the castle's dungeon."

"I understand," Bronn said, following Olvard's guards. "At least it's warm there."

Olvard led Deanna and Derek through the castle's corridors to Bronn's office where they found the glowing green vial. They raced back to find Telgaar who was in the Royal Garden, talking to a particularly pretty purple flower.

"Uncle," Olvard said softly.

Telgaar turned away from the flower. "Ah, Olvard." He stopped for a second. "There's something different about you. Is it a new haircut? No, you don't have hair."

"I've become a Red Dragon, like the last great king before me," Olvard said.

Telgaar looked at him and smiled with a distant memory of his time as king. "That was a long time ago," Telgaar said.

"Not so long," Olvard replied, handing the vial to his uncle. "Open it."

Telgaar looked confused, but unscrewed the top. He looked down into the misty green energy. Slowly, fingers of green flame oozed out of the vial and swirled around the former king. When all of the energy was absorbed into his body, he breathed deeply. The first change was a fire in his eyes. It was like he woke up from years of sleep. Then, his skin began to turn orange and then red. His arms puffed up, and he grew taller.

When the transformation was complete, Telgaar was nearly the same size as Olvard. "You have saved me," Telgaar said.

Olvard looked at his friends, and said, "It was a team effort." He looked back toward his uncle and said, "There is so much that you have to teach me."

"And there is apparently much that you need to teach me," Telgaar said.

"Excuse me," Deanna interrupted, with a troubled look coming across her face. "I hope you don't mind my asking, but how did they steal your power? You were the strongest dragon in the Realm."

"That is a good question," Telgaar said. "I did not know that I had enemies who were powerful enough to do this to me so quickly."

"Do you know who may have done it?" she asked.

"I'm afraid not," Telgaar answered. "The last thing that I can remember was that I was meeting with one of my dearest friends."

"Was he a dragon from the Realm?" Deanna asked.

"No, he wasn't a dragon at all," Telgaar said.

"He was a wizard from outside the Dragon Realms."

Derek and Deanna looked at each other. "Was it Iszarre?" Derek asked, wondering if their friend had something to do with Telgaar's overthrow.

"No, no, I've heard of Iszarre, but I don't think he ever came to my castle," Telgaar replied. Derek sighed, relieved. "No, my friend's name was Eldrack."

The silence stretched as Derek, Deanna, and Olvard tried to recover from the shock of learning that Telgaar had known Eldrack and had let the dark wizard freely enter his castle.

Zorell stared at Telgaar with deep concern in his eyes, but he said nothing. Tobungus watched Zorell and sensed something confusing in his feline nemesis. Zorell walked out of the room, with Tobungus right behind him.

"Eldrack did this to you??" Deanna said, thinking that she finally had proof that Eldrack really was evil.

"Eldrack did what?" Telgaar asked.

"This," Derek cut in, waving his hands toward Telgaar. "He stole your power so that Bronn and the Outfliers could take over."

"Why would he do that?" Telgaar asked.

"Eldrack was my friend."

"You don't know, do you?" Deanna said quietly.

"Know what?" Telgaar asked.

"Oh, boy," Derek whispered. "You better sit down for this."

Telgaar was still a bit dizzy from his transformation, so he made himself comfortable against a wall near a large fountain and waited to hear Derek's story.

"Telgaar," Derek began, "Eldrack has become a dark wizard, and he's trying to overthrow King Barado and conquer all of Elestra."

"That's impossible," Telgaar said. "I have known Eldrack for a very long time, and I never saw him do anything like that. There must be some mistake."

"You may have known the old Eldrack," Deanna said quietly, "but something happened to him, and he is evil. He grew powerful enough to stop the magic from flowing in Amemnop, and he has captured thirteen generations of our family."

"Why would he want to capture your family?" Telgaar asked.

"We are Mystical Guardians. Eldrack knows that our family would stand in his way."

"You're Mystical Guardians?" Telgaar said in

deeper disbelief. "Then, you should know," but he didn't finish his thought.

"We should know what?" Derek asked quickly.

"Never mind," Telgaar answered. "I'm still very tired, and I must not be thinking straight."

Derek and Deanna both felt uneasy with Telgaar's sudden change. They wondered what he was going to say and why he decided not to tell them. Derek could not stop himself, and blurted out, "Telgaar, is there something else that you know about Eldrack?"

Telgaar stared at the fountain for a long time, and then said slowly. "No, I don't think so." He paused again. "Sometimes, we learn that there are very few people we can really trust. Of course, I trust Olvard and you two because you had the choice to keep the vial and not help me, but you did. There is only one other friend that I trust like that and that was a boy I knew when I was a child. We met in the mountains and played endlessly. There was an attack on the kingdom, and he helped me hide, even though that was very dangerous for him. When I told him that I didn't want to get him in trouble, he told me that I had to grow up and become a great king. He kept telling me that Elestra needed leaders who would make things better for everyone."

"What happened to your friend?" Deanna asked nervously. She wondered if the boy had been caught helping Telgaar.

"I don't know," Telgaar said. "Maybe, I'll try to find him now that I am back to my old self."

"We will need your help," Deanna said. "The battle is getting more intense every day."

"I feel that," Telgaar said. "There is something different in the air. A dark wind is blowing through Elestra."

"That's Eldrack," Derek said.

"Perhaps. Perhaps, you are correct," Telgaar said. "I thought Eldrack was my friend, but now I must try to figure out what happened."

10 The Dark Night

Derek and Deanna found Tobungus and Zorell resting in the courtyard. They seemed too tired from their adventure to insult each other, and sat quietly against the stone fountain.

"Come on, guys," Deanna called as she walked through the massive archway. Her friends nodded and slowly got to their feet.

"Let's go," Tobungus said to Zorell, "and try not to shed. We're in a palace, after all." Derek and Deanna shared a smile. The truce was finally over.

"I'd worry more about your spores clogging the air and making the dragons sneeze," Zorell replied.

Deanna stared at them and slowly pulled the wand out. Not wanting to end up in the cold waters of the fountain, they both stopped their bantering and hurried to join her.

Olvard asked Deanna if she would allow him to fly all of them to the edge of the Dragon Realm. They climbed onto his back, and he took off. He flew up high through the clouds and then low over the town around his castle.

As other dragons saw their red king soaring above them, they took flight to fly with him. Before long, dozens of dragons were flying like a huge squadron of fighter planes. The group made their way back to the area where Derek and Deanna had first entered the Dragon Realm.

Olvard landed next to the path and helped everyone down. His followers were forming huge circles above him, with bursts of flames to show their excitement.

"Thank you, Olvard," Deanna said. "I hope we can come back to visit you again soon."

"I would love another visit from you two." He looked at Zorell and Tobungus and corrected himself, "I mean, I would love another visit from the four of you."

"This adventure couldn't have been any better. We were able to watch you turn into the Red Dragon," Tobungus said to Olvard. Turning to Zorell, he added, "And, we visited the Elestran paradise known as the Torallian Forest."

The cat sighed. "Oh, don't worry, Zorell. We'll be going back through again, in case you missed any of the finer details of my homeland."

"Yippee, I can't wait for that," Zorell replied.

Olvard laughed at Zorell and Tobungus, and said, "Now, I must go. I will gather a large force of dragons to face the Outfliers. My guess, and my hope, is that they will give up easily, and we can then have peace in the Dragon Realms."

"I hope you are right," Derek said. "If you need help, please send for us."

"That I will," Olvard said, as he flapped his wings and took to the skies.

The trip back to the Torallian Forest was quick, and they did not run into any problems along the way.

Their journey through the Torallian Forest, however, was not as quick as Zorell would have liked. Bohootus had heard about their work in the Dragon Realm and had organized a parade in their honor.

Tobungus changed into his new slippers, which caught the attention of a large group of young mushroom people. They huddled around him, admiring his fuzzy slippers and asking where he found such wondrous creations.

Tobungus smiled and said, "Now, now, children. You'll all get a chance to pet my new slippers."

As the parade started, a strange noise filled the air. Derek and Deanna had never heard Torallian music before, and they weren't sure they would be attending another concert anytime soon.

The first musical group rode on a float in the parade. Half of them smashed huge glass tubes, while the other half set off firecrackers in metal cans. "A fine Torallian symphony," Tobungus whispered.

Derek looked sideways at Tobungus to see if he was joking. He wasn't.

The next band played a gorgeous piece of music that sounded like it had been played by the finest orchestra. Tobungus turned up his nose and said, "teenagers and their noise."

"You can't be serious," Deanna said. "That music is beautiful."

"Oh, Deanna, we must expose you to much more Torallian music so that you can fully appreciate the great works of my people," Tobungus replied.

Before Deanna could say anything, Tobungus held up his hand. "Shh, here come the bagpipers."

A group of at least four hundred mushroom people playing bagpipes passed them. Derek and Deanna were surprised that the pipers were all playing together, instead of just making as much irritating noise as possible.

"Okay, that was impressive," Derek said.

The parade wound down, and the group set off once again for Amemnop. Zorell was getting happier and happier as they came closer to the end of their trip. The twins knew that travelling through the Torallian Forest twice had driven him crazy.

When they got to Glabber's, Zorell said that he would be back later, after he visited a friend across town. Tobungus sat out on the wooden walkway in front of the diner and shined his many shoes in the fading sunlight.

The twins stopped inside to tell Glabber that they would be back in about an hour, after they took the moonstone to the Tower of the Moons. He promised to have a huge meal waiting for them, so they set off with thoughts of a delicious, but strange dinner.

The sun had completely set when they had gotten halfway to the Tower, and the moons were already shining brightly. They walked slowly, looking into the windows of the shops that they passed and talking about their time with Olvard and Telgaar.

They were enjoying the peaceful walk so much that they almost missed a change in the sky. One of the faintest moons had gone dark. The others were so bright that it was hardly noticeable. A second moon went dark as Deanna glanced upward.

"Derek," she said, "I think one of the moons just disappeared."

Derek looked up and strained to see the moon that should have shone brightly above them. He could barely see it. It looked like a moon that was blocked by an eclipse. But the sun had just gone down, and the moon was directly overhead, so he knew that it was not being blocked by an eclipse.

As he thought about what this could mean, Deanna said, "There are only thirteen moons shining right now." As she finished, they both saw a third moon becoming dimmer.

"It looks like something is blocking the moons' light," Derek said. "We'd better hurry and look through the moonstone."

As Deanna dug in her pocket for the moonstone, Derek said, "Hurry up, another moon just disappeared."

"Got it," Deanna said. She looked up and saw that the fifth moon was starting to get dim. She held the moonstone up and looked through it. Derek looked over her shoulder, not waiting until she was finished.

They both felt the rush of magical energy wash over them. They had looked through the moonstone in the nick of time.

"That was too close," Derek said. "I think we

should get to the Tower as fast as we can. If Eldrack's spell of darkness has returned, we should get this moonstone in the arch before we face him."

"Yeah, we don't want there to be any chance that he could steal the stone from us," Deanna said.

They ran the rest of the way to the Tower, and took the steps two at a time. They were panting by the time they reached the top. Deanna quickly snapped the moonstone into the arch.

They stepped back and looked at the sky. The last of the moons were being covered by the dark veil. Moments later, all fifteen moons were dark.

Deanna looked into the pitch black Elestra night, toward the houses and shops below. Through the darkness, she saw a pair of orange eyes on the top floor of a building across the square from the Tower. The eyes seemed to stare deep into her mind, and then they blinked and were gone. The moons emerged from the darkness, and the night was lit up by their brilliance.

"Looks like someone knows we got here in time," Derek said.

"He came here, Derek," Deanna said. "Amemnop is growing stronger every day, and Eldrack still was able to come here, almost all the way to the Tower. He's getting braver."

"Or more worried that we'll find all of the moonstones," Derek said.

"I suppose you're right," Deanna replied. "We've found the first five, and he hasn't been able to stop us. I wonder if that means he'll bring more of his allies or attack us when we don't expect it next time."

"We'll just have to be even more careful," Derek said.

The Fifth Vision

"Last time we put a moonstone into the Arch, we forgot to look through it to see the vision," Deanna said. "Let's not make that same mistake again."

"Yeah, and since Glabber's going to have a big meal for us, I'd rather be done here at the Tower so we can eat and then get some sleep," Derek said.

They lined up the fifth moon through the moonstone and put their heads together to see the vision.

Something was wrong. They were not transported to the temple inside the pit of Mt. Infernus. They only saw the image of a huge black dragon. It just stood there and stared at them. They tried to look around in their vision, but wherever they looked, the black dragon blocked their view.

Derek and Deanna backed away from the Arch and looked at each other. "What was that all about?" Derek asked.

"I don't know," Deanna said. "That's the first time that we've had trouble seeing the vision."

"I wonder if it has anything to do with

Eldrack making the moons dark," Derek said.

Deanna thought about the eyes that stared into her mind. She closed her eyes and thought about why Eldrack might have dared to come to Amemnop. She had thought that he was trying to look into her mind to see what they had done in the Dragon Realms, but then she realized that he was really trying to put a thought into her mind.

"Derek, Eldrack planted the image of the Black Dragon in my mind," Deanna said. "He's trying to block us from seeing the vision.

"How do we stop him?" Derek asked.

"We need to look again," Deanna said. "But, this time, we have to imagine that we are pushing the Black Dragon away." She saw that he didn't understand what she meant, so she added, "Just trust me. We have to imagine that we are using our minds to fight the Black Dragon."

They looked through the moonstone again, and the Black Dragon returned. This time, they imagined that they were sending waves of magical energy at the Black Dragon. The Black Dragon began to flap its wings like a bird fighting against the wind trying to blow it off of a branch.

They saw that they were winning, so they pushed harder with their minds. The Black Dragon opened its mouth and sent a blast of icy wind at them, but Derek imagined a shield of fire that melted the ice. At the same time, Deanna imagined a blast of fire that shot out of Derek's shield and hit the Black Dragon. Their enemy fell backward and shrunk until it disappeared.

The steam from their battle swirled, and when it lifted, they were standing on one of the floating rocks in the magma outside of the temple. They looked up and saw a purple dragon with orange wings carrying an old man who was probably Barndoble, the fifth Mystical Guardian. There were at least a dozen other purple dragons flying close behind them.

Barndoble yelled over the sounds of the beating wings, "You four stay out here and keep him from entering the temple. We'll go inside and complete the mission."

Four of the purple dragons looped around and flew in circles over the magma. The rest of the dragons flew through the gate to the temple.

Derek and Deanna could feel the heat from the magma and the rushing wind from the flying dragons, but they could also sense fear in the purple dragons.

They looked up and saw a dark figure standing on the rim of the volcano. It was Eldrack. He held his arms out and dove down into the volcano's pit. As he fell, he transformed into a shimmering black dragon.

The four purple dragons moved together to attack Eldrack, but he was so fast that their fiery jets missed him. He breathed blasts of ice at them and quickly knocked them all aside.

"We need to see inside the temple," Deanna said. Instantly, they were inside the temple where they saw Barndoble's dragon hovering next to the huge guard statue's arm. He looked back as the black dragon burst through the gate.

The purple dragons prepared to attack the black dragon, but Barndoble yelled, "No! You must escape. Eldrack's coming for me. The rest of you get to safety and get a message to King Barado about this attack."

The dragon that Barndoble was riding set him down in front of the statue and then followed the other purple dragons as they soared straight up. There was a tunnel that would lead back to the main chamber and allow them to escape. The black dragon watched the purple dragons disappear into the tunnel and turned toward Barndoble with an icy smile across his scaly face.

Barndoble drew his wand and waited. The black dragon landed on the statue's platform and transformed   back   into   Eldrack.   Barndoble immediately fired a blast of magical energy at Eldrack and knocked him backward into the magma.

Barndoble looked shocked. Had he just beaten Eldrack? He didn't stay confused long. The black dragon exploded out of the magma and fired a wave of ice at Barndoble.

The Mystical Guardian was frozen solid. The black dragon picked him up and flew up to the tunnel that the purple dragons had used.

The vision faded.

"You've got to be kidding me," Derek said. "He can transform into a dragon."

"This adds a fun new twist to Eldrack," Deanna said.

"Hey, Deanna," Derek said, "could this be the new type of magic that Eldrack used when Baladorn almost captured him?"

"Oh, you mean that maybe he transformed into something else and escaped," she said.

"Yeah," Derek replied. "It didn't have to be a dragon. Maybe he changed into a squirrel and just skittered away. No one would have suspected that a little animal was Eldrack, so he could have slipped past Baladorn's army."

"That would be an effective trick," Deanna said. "That might explain how he was able to come into Amemnop tonight without people seeing him."

"We should definitely ask Iszarre about this," Derek said.

"Speaking of Iszarre, we should get back to the Grub Hut for that special meal that Glabber's making," Deanna said.

They hurried back down the stairs and into the warm Amemnop night. They walked quickly to Glabber's and sat down at a table that was covered with a rainbow of foods, or more accurately, rainbows of foods.

"Welcome back," Glabber said. "I've set up a special feast for you tonight. I figure a celebration is in order, since you recovered the moonstone and rescued King Telgaar."

"What is all this?" Derek asked, pointing to the small rainbows that arched from one end of the table to the other. Each rainbow had plates of food of certain colors hovering in midair, waiting for the twins to decide what they would eat.

"The first rainbow has small things to start your meal," Glabber said. "I think you call them appetizers."

"And it's all very appetizing," Iszarre's voice cut in. "The other rainbows have soups, main dishes, pizzas, and desserts."

"Uh, oh!" Deanna said, looking at Derek.

"These soups won't set your allergy off, will they?"

"I think the soup allergy's gone," Derek said. "Rorrdoogo said that the allergy would turn into a super allergy for a while and then disappear. It seemed really powerful when we were over the magma soup, but now, I don't feel anything."

"That's good," Deanna said, turning her attention to the food in front of her. "This is incredible." She and Derek tried one crazy dish after another. Soon, they were stuffed and ready to talk to Iszarre about their trip to the Dragon Realms.

"You two had quite an adventure in the Dragon Realm, I hear," Iszarre said. "But, it's interesting that Eldrack didn't follow you there and try to take the moonstone from you."

"Well, we saw him in the Torallian Forest," Derek said. "And, Bronn and the other dragons who were planning on betraying Olvard worked with Eldrack. He probably didn't think he needed to be there."

"I doubt that," Iszarre said. "He's seen how powerful you are. I don't think that he would believe that a few dragons without magical powers could stand up to you."

Derek laughed. "I'm sorry, Iszarre, but that just sounds so strange. Not long ago, we would never have believed that a group of huge dragons wouldn't be able to defeat us."

"I know that it will take a while to get used to your power here in Elestra," Iszarre explained. "But, never assume that you know why Eldrack is doing anything. Always keep your eyes open and your minds sharp."

"Okay, since you said that," Deanna said, "We saw a strange vision when we looked through the fifth moonstone. First, Eldrack was trying to block us by putting up an image of a black dragon. Then, we saw that he actually turned into the black dragon when he captured Barndoble."

"Yes, Eldrack has mastered transformation," Iszarre said. "Strong wizards are able to do that."

"So transforming is not the unknown type of magic that he used against Baladorn?" Deanna said.

"What's that over there," Iszarre said, pointing to the door. The twins saw nothing and turned back to Iszarre, but he had disappeared. In his place, a colorful parrot stood on the back of a chair.

The parrot squawked and said, "See, I turned myself into an eagle."

"Um, you're not an eagle," Deanna said.

"What?" the bird screeched. It flapped its wings clumsily and bounced over to the counter where Glabber was coiled up. "Glabber, am I an eagle?"

"You look like an eagle to me," the snake said.

"Ha!" the parrot said, before transforming back into Iszarre. "Apparently you two need to learn what an eagle looks like."

"Yeah, sure," Derek said. "We'll work on that whole eagle/parrot thing. But, at least we know that Eldrack's not the only wizard who can transform."

"No, certainly not," Iszarre said. "You two will learn how to transform at some point."

"Maybe we can turn into eagles too," Derek said, while giving Deanna a sideways look.

"Derek, how could we forget that Bohootus transformed when we were in the Torallian Forest?" Deanna said.

"Ah, yes. The fearsome panda," Derek replied. "If Bohootus can transform, it must not be that hard."

"Don't underestimate Bohootus," Iszarre said. "I've worked with him many times, and he is much stronger than you might believe."

"That is surprising," Deanna murmured. "But, since we learned that Eldrack can disguise himself as other creatures, we need to focus on making our magic more powerful before our next quest."

"Oh my, look at the time," Iszarre said.

"What do you mean?" Derek said. "Are you trying to change the subject?"

"Not at all, Derek," Iszarre answered. "I'm just saying that you should look at the time, and keep looking at it. You may be surprised that it's earlier when it seems like it should be later."

"Very cryptic," Deanna said. "What does watching the time have to do with our next quest?"

"Nothing and everything," Iszarre replied. "Oh, and pack a raincoat. I hear it's misty this time of year in the Forest Kingdom."

"The Forest Kingdom is a big place," Deanna said. "You're usually a bit more specific, when you give us hints about our next adventures."

"I've already given you the only hint you'll need," Iszarre said. "Time is a funny thing here in Elestra."

Turn the page. The adventure continues…

Epilogue

Derek and Deanna have now found five moonstones and defeated Eldrack and his minions in Amemnop, the Atteelian Orchard, and the Desert Realm, on Mt. Drasius, and in the pit of Mt. Infernus, but there is much more to do and much more to learn.

In their bits of free time, Deanna and Derek continue to wander through the State Library of Magia to find out more about the places, people, and creatures they have encountered. The following pages will tell you what they learned, or perhaps what they didn't learn.

Purple Dragons

The next morning, Derek and Deanna grabbed a quick breakfast and hurried to the library. Eldrack's appearance in Amemnop the night before made them nervous, and they wanted to be prepared for their next meeting with him.

Deanna asked the librarian for books about the purple dragons, and the usual wave of excited book fairies zoomed out from under the desk and raced to grab the books that were lit up on the shelves above them. Derek and Deanna had agreed that they should read about the purple dragons because Olvard had explained that dragon wizards were purple. They saw a group of purple dragons battling Eldrack in their vision, but when they were at Olvard's castle, they hadn't seen any purple dragons. They had also seen a purple dragon in a mural inside the pyramid where they found the third moonstone. They wanted to know what had happened to the purple dragons after the battle inside Mt. Infernus.

A small stack of books stood in front of them on their table. "Well, here goes," Deanna said, as she pulled out the wand. She pointed it at a book titled *Wizards in the Southern Elestran Lands*, and said, *"Explanatum."*

The book shivered and opened its cover dramatically.

"I'd like to know about the purple dragons," Deanna said. "Are all dragon wizards purple?"

The book flipped past its introduction, and settled on the middle of the first chapter. A voice that sounded like it came from someone with a very bad cold said,

> *Dragon wizards go through a series of tests to prove that they have mastered the types of magic that dragons can use. If a dragon passes these tests, he becomes purple. Like all dragons, the color that they become indicates their power.*
>
> *Kings can become yellow, orange, or red, if they are truly powerful. All dragon wizards become purple, but the strongest have orange wings. There are legends of dragon wizards with other rare color combinations, but no one can confirm that these strangely colored dragons ever existed.*
>
> *Dragons who have not yet taken the magical tests are green like normal dragons. They can use magic, but their abilities are weak.*

Dragons who fail the tests remain green and cannot gain great power until they go back and pass the tests. Dragons who want to be wizards but fail the tests often can only use magic effectively if they use magical items to boost their power.

The book stopped reading for a few moments and then said, "Is there anything else that I can help you with?"

"Hmm," Deanna said. "Just a second." She turned to Derek to ask him if he had any questions for the book, but she saw that he was staring across the library. He stood up and slowly began walking toward the librarian's desk. "Derek," she said, but he didn't seem to hear her.

Deanna got up to see if he was alright. She noticed that he walked right past the librarian's desk, and was heading for a spiral staircase that led down into the depths below the library.

Deanna hurried to catch up with Derek, but the tiny fairy librarian zipped up from her desk and floated in front of Deanna's face. "I'm sorry, Deanna, but Derek has been called by Gula Badu," the librarian said. "You must wait for him up here."

"Oh," Deanna said, still watching her brother walk along as if he were in a trance. "I guess I'll go back and look at some of the other books."

* *

Derek climbed down through the levels underneath the library. As he got closer to the Archive of Prophecies, his mind began to clear. He knew that Gula Badu had called to him and pulled him to her, and he felt the urgency in her call.

He wasn't scared of the dark, damp corridor this time. He walked quickly and was ready to knock on the door, when it opened with a very predictable creaking sound. "Come in, Derek," the ancient voice said.

Derek looked at the rows of unlit candles lining the walls and the cauldron of green flame in the center of the room. This hidden chamber was frightening the first time he had entered it, but now it seemed like being called here was a signal that he was growing more powerful.

"I came to see you before we went to the Dragon Realms, but the librarian said that you were away," Derek said.

"Yes," Gula Badu whispered slowly. "I am older than you can imagine, and sometimes I have to go to the Antikrom Mountains to get younger."

"To get younger?" Derek asked.

"Yes, Derek," Gula Badu said, laughing slightly. "I have already told you that there are some wizards who experience time in reverse. There are also a few places where time itself is backwards. If you go to one of these places, you can become younger. I make these trips to a very special place where time flows very quickly in reverse. I do this so that I can survive to protect the prophecies."

Derek wasn't sure what to say because he didn't really understand how time could go backwards. He sounded confused when he said, "Is there a prophecy that you wanted me to see?"

"Yes, yes," Gula Badu said, shuffling to the wall to Derek's right. She struggled to reach a candle that was hidden behind a few others. When she had it in her hands, she lit it and set it in front of Derek.

Derek remembered what he had to do. He stared into the candle's green flame and saw the words floating in between the flickering flame and the wisps of smoke. The prophecy said,

> The Dragon Realms saw war and then peace.
> The great Red Dragon King united the Sky Dragons from all of the realms into one

powerful, peaceful Realm.

The King wanted great wizards by his side, and many dragons trained to serve the mighty Telgaar.

The fifty most powerful purple dragons were chosen to form the king's Army of the Purple Wind.

The cloud of darkness that set over Elestra swallowed the Purple Wizards one by one.

When only the strongest remained, a dragon that never existed defeated and captured the others.

No one knows where they went, only that in the darkest hour, they will return, but only if the Light of Dentarus splits and rejoins on the field of battle.

When the prophecy ended, Derek looked down and saw the words written on a piece of paper on the table in front of him. He picked the paper up and read the prophecy to himself again. He thought that he understood some of it, but not all of it.

Gula Badu saw his uncertainty. "You will have plenty of time to learn what the prophecy means, young Derek," she said. "Your sister is waiting for you upstairs."

Derek folded the paper and put it in his pocket. When he left the room, he turned to say goodbye to the old woman.

"We will see each other again many times," Gula Badu said. "And, I look forward to the day when all of these prophecies are realized."

"Why do I feel like your words are another prophecy?" Derek asked.

"Perhaps they are," she answered. "I spend most of my days surrounded by these prophecies. I suppose I tend to sound like them once in a while."

Derek thought about her words and headed back up the spiral staircase to the library's main hall. He found Deanna sitting at the same table, talking to a book that was telling her that the library could be a scary place at night because the snoring of the book fairies sounded like the roars of Barokan fire bats.

Deanna looked up and said, "Are you feeling better?"

"What do you mean?" Derek replied. Then he realized that he probably looked like a zombie walking to the Archive earlier. "Oh, yeah, all better now. Gula Badu had another prophecy for me to see." He pulled the paper out of his pocket and said, "Here, read it for yourself."

Deanna read through the prophecy and said,

"Hmm. I read something about Army of the Purple Wind while you were down there. This looks like it's about the time when Eldrack defeated the purple dragons."

"Yeah," Derek said, "But, that part about the Light of Dentarus isn't really clear yet."

"I'm sure we'll figure it out," Deanna added. "It doesn't seem like this prophecy talks about us joining Eldrack. That's a good thing."

"But, remember, Deanna, all of these prophecies have us in them," Derek said. "We're obviously not purple dragons, so that part about the Light of Dentarus is probably about us." He saw that Deanna was thinking through what he said. "And, I don't really like the part about the light splitting."

"But, Derek, it says that the light rejoins after that," Deanna said.

"Okay, Deanna, we're just guessing here," Derek said. "I'm starving. Let's get something to eat and come back this afternoon."

The Black Dragon

Derek and Deanna walked toward the River of Serenity, where they had seen rows of food stands on an earlier walk. They passed cafes and restaurants along the way, but they wanted to stretch their lunch break. Reading a prophecy about themselves always made them feel exhausted. The last thing they wanted right then was to fight with a stubborn book about giving up its information.

They ordered little bits of food from six different vendors and then settled into spots on the short stone wall next to the river. They ate slowly and let the peaceful flow of the water calm their minds.

They both knew when it was time to return to the library, and they headed back refreshed. The library was very quiet when they entered. They looked around, but saw no one else in the main hall.

Deanna went to the librarian's desk and asked for books about the black dragon.

"The black dragon?" the librarian said.

"Yes," Deanna said. "We want to learn about the black dragon."

"I'm sorry, young lady, but there are no books on a black dragon," the librarian said.

Deanna heard a faint noise that she couldn't identify. She looked around, but could not figure out where it was coming from. "Okay, then how about books about dragons with unusual colors. I heard that there are legends about oddly colored dragons."

"Yes, I know just the book you will need," the librarian said. She called out to one book fairy and told her to retrieve *Legends of the Rainbow Dragons*. The book fairy shot up to a book about halfway up the library's back wall and carried a book to the table where Derek was already sitting.

Deanna had the wand out when she sat down. *"Explanatum,"* she said. "We would like to know about oddly colored dragons."

The book was excited to read to the twins. The books all knew that they came in and got stacks of books to learn about Elestra. This book was the only one they chose on this visit, so it felt very special. An eager voice said,

All dragons are born green. Throughout their lives, they can change colors, if they are kings, wizards, or chefs. There are a few dragons who are not kings or wizards but still change colors. Most dragons that are uniquely colored spend a lot of time outside the Dragon Realms

and eat strange foods that make them take on strange colors. Some are solid colors. Others have wings of different colors. Some have stripes or colorful patches. These rare dragons can be any color of the rainbow.

The book stopped reading and said, "Is that helpful?"

"Yes," Deanna said. "We had no idea how dragons got their colors, except for the kings and wizards."

"But, what we'd really like to know is about black dragons," Derek added.

"Oh, my," the book said, "There are no black dragons. Dragons cannot be black, white, or gray. Those colors are outside of the colors in the rainbow."

"But, we've seen," Derek started, but Deanna grabbed his arm to stop him.

"How about this?" Deanna started. "Are there any legends about black dragons? I know that they would not be true, but we're just looking for stories." Deanna heard the same faint sound, but still could not find its source.

"Well, there is a legend about a magical black dragon that appeared and defeated an army of purple dragons before vanishing into thin air," the book said.

"Are there any more details about this black dragon," Deanna asked.

"I'm sorry, but no," the book said. "If I may say so, it is almost like the person who wrote the story was afraid to add any more information."

The faint noise was a bit louder, and Derek heard it this time as well. "What is that sound?" he asked.

"I don't know," Deanna replied. "It sounds almost like someone is laughing quietly."

They continued to look around the library, when something caught Derek's eye. The single book on the Shelf of Isolation moved slightly. "Up there," he said, pointing at the book.

They both looked at the book and were able to hear it more clearly. "Do you think that book knows something about the black dragon?" Deanna whispered.

Derek didn't answer. He was concentrating on the book that was laughing more loudly now, almost as if it were teasing them. Suddenly, the book began laughing so that anyone could hear it.

Before the twins could decide what to do, Iszarre burst into the library and said, "Derek, Deanna, we must leave. Eldrack is here in Amemnop."

Preview of Book 6

Derek and Deanna seek the sixth moonstone in *The Misty Peaks of Dentarus*. We usually like to include the first chapter of the next book as a preview, but there are just a few too many secrets in Chapter 1 of the next book. Will Eldrack and his followers succeed in storming the Tower of the Moons? What new kind of magic has Deanna discovered without using the Wand of Ondarell? How much will Tobungus brag to Zorell about fighting an army of giant spiders? And, that's just Chapter 1.

Derek and Deanna travel to the Forest Kingdom where they visit the Antikrom Mountains where time flows backward. Whether they know it or not, one of their most important discoveries is a simple yak farmer who lives high in the secluded mountains.

Peekaboo Pepper Books

The line-up of Peekaboo Pepper Books is expanding quickly. We would like to take this opportunity to provide short previews of other titles in the *Guardians of Elestra* series.

The Dark City: Guardians of Elestra #1

Deanna and Derek follow their grandfather to Elestra where they learn that they are the last hope against a dark wizard in a race to collect the magical moonstones. They'll need all the help they can get from Tobungus, the tap-dancing mushroom man, Iszarre, the powerful wizard/fry cook, and Glabber, the snake wizard. Talking books, book fairies, flying coyote birdmen, devious hot peppers, and a short-tempered frog make their first adventure in Elestra one to remember.

The Giants of the Baroka Valley: Guardians of Elestra #2

Deanna and Derek set out on their second adventure in Elestra with Tobungus the mushroom man at their side. Along the way, they meet Zorell, a cat who has a hate/hate relationship with Tobungus, and ride a giant goose to the Baroka Valley. In the land where everything is huge, from the plants and animals to the grains of sand on a beach, they face off against Eldrack, fend off some sickening gong music, and sail down the River of the Dragon's Breath on an unusual boat. In the end, they are left with a new mystery and a plate of panpies (er, pancakes).

The Desert of the Crescent Dunes: Guardians of Elestra #3

Derek and Deanna venture outside of Magia for the first time. They find the Desert Realm to be hot and filled with Eldrack's minions. Their new friend Zorell joins them on the trip, much to Tobungus' dismay. It's a good thing he does, because his dancing proves to be a powerful weapon against Eldrack's army of tentacled sand beasts. Fortunately, the Desert Realm isn't without friends. They meet a resourceful girl named Dahlia who feeds them sugary lizard tails and reads prophecies woven in a hidden tapestry. After finding the entrance to a secret desert, they run into a mysterious statue who points out a solution to their problem. To escape from Eldrack's reach and return the moonstone to the arch, they must cross the Great Snort Pit in a boat scarred with bite marks that are frighteningly large.

The Seven Pillars of Tarook: Guardians of Elestra #4

Mount Drasius is cold, very cold, unless you're on the side with the flowing lava. For Derek and Deanna, and their travel partners Tobungus and Zorell, the journey is to the cold side of the mountain. They team up with a band of snowball-throwing kangaroos living near a great temple that just might be the hiding place of the fourth moonstone. Eldrack's magic looks strong enough to finally defeat the twins, until a pair of sweaty socks powers up Deanna's magic.

The Misty Peaks of Dentarus: Guardians of Elestra #6

A trip to the mountains would be a nice way for Derek and Deanna to relax after their first five encounters with Eldrack. Unfortunately, these are the Antikrom Mountains where time occasionally goes in reverse, and where valleys are perfect places for an ambush by Eldrack's forces. The Iron Forest floats above the highest peaks, and the twins learn that sometimes the right jacket is all you need to fly. They meet their uncle, the yak farmer who insists that he must stay out of the family's battle against Eldrack. That's too bad because he could tip balance in their favor.

Author Bio

Thom Jones is the author of the *Guardians of Elestra* series, as well as two forthcoming series, *Galactic Gourmets* (science fiction) and *The Adventures of Boron Jones* (superhero meets chemistry).

He has taught subjects including history, atmospheric science, and criminology at various colleges. What he loves to do most, though, is work with kids, which he does at the crime scene camps he runs. He began writing the *Guardians of Elestra* stories in 2004 for his two sons. The stories evolved, and Tobungus got stranger over the years. He finally decided to start Peekaboo Pepper Books and publish the stories with the view that kids are smart and funny, and that they are more engaged by somewhat challenging vocabulary and mysteries woven throughout the stories they read.

He lives in the Adirondacks with his wife Linda and their three children, Galen, Aidan, and Dinara. He is extremely lucky to have such wonderful editors in Linda, Galen, and Aidan, who have found too many errors to count and have come up with fantastic ideas, even when they don't know it.